Tough Job in Driftwood

Tough Job in Driftwood

WESTERN STORIES

Richard Prosch

WHEELER PUBLISHING
A part of Gale, a Cengage Company

These stories are works of fiction. Places and incidents are the product of the author's imagination or in the case of actual locations, are used fictitiously. Any similarity to any persons, living or dead, past, present or future is coincidental.

Wheeler Publishing Large Print Softcover Western.
The text of this Large Print edition is unabridged.
Other aspects of the book may vary from the original edition.
Set in 16 pt. Plantin.

**LIBRARY OF CONGRESS CIP DATA ON FILE.
CATALOGUING IN PUBLICATION FOR THIS BOOK
IS AVAILABLE FROM THE LIBRARY OF CONGRESS.**

ISBN-13: 978-1-4328-9978-3 (softcover alk. paper)

Published in 2022 by arrangement with Richard Prosch

Printed in the United States of America
2 3 4 5 6   27 26 25 24 23

TABLE OF CONTENTS

For Wayne D. Dundee

Who knows from crime and western stories and about friendship and caring

Tough Job in Driftwood

The faces under the yellow electric lights were old and young. Czech and Pole. German and Swede. Men and boys. A couple wives and mothers.

The professional gals hung out in the corner by the oak beer barrel under the portrait of Roosevelt.

Probably three dozen people in the crowd.

All of them covered with a thin layer of Sandhills grit. Just like everything else for miles around. Outside in the dirt parking lot a few cackling motor cars rolled in. Most folks still came by horse and wagon.

All in all, a good showing for the Broke Horse Barn on a hot Nebraska night.

From the rickety pine board bandstand Carson scanned the crowd in vain. He'd know the man when he saw him

A man for a tough job needed doing.

But nobody in the crowd was the one Carson wanted.

Carson finished his cigarette and gave the sloppy gal up front a wink. Then pitching the butt to the sawdust and tobacco spit covered floor, he swung his guitar around on its sweaty chafing strap.

Even his bushy blonde mustache dripped from the heat.

Behind him Bald Billy, the only colored man around for a hundred miles in any direction, jerked a bass chord.

To the right Lanky Dirk tapped the cow bell.

In the peaked pine barn rafters far above, two pigeons flapped their wings, dusting the night owls below with bits of straw and dirt-dobber nests. "Let's go," the birds seemed to say.

Down at the depot, the midnight express blew a farewell whistle while the sloppy gal hooked a thread of a strap back over her shoulder and slid off to a booth, melting into a cowboy's lap under a naked light bulb.

"One, two, three," said Carson.

Rearing back so far that his Stetson threatened to fall off his head, Carson tore into the strings of "Dad's Night Out" with a blurry hand.

It didn't sound right.

But the Swedes in the horse stalls started

clapping anyway, and a couple boys in back lifted their beer mugs high with a "Yaa-hoo."

They came to Driftwood with the rail, for the women, for the adventure. They came to Driftwood to prove they were cattlemen, or gunmen, or gamblers.

Some came just to say they'd been there.

Nobody came to make it a home.

First out on the dance floor, Fat Irma, dragged her husband, Burt, by his ear before swinging him around by the wrist.

Carson grinned and kept at the guitar strings hard, like he was scratching a scaly red itch.

When they hit the bridge, Irma broke loose.

Pale white skin flapping like laundry above her raw red elbows, and her flour sack dress hitching up in back, she was a force of nature, thundering through the growing crowd. Burt pumped his boney knees up and down. When they swung each other around, Carson held his breath.

Surely one of them would crash into the bandstand.

But neither of them did.

Folks in Driftwood had their own way of moving.

Less organized than a square dance, but

more formal than the loosey-goosey shit that passed for dancing in the city, these impromptu promenades and thundering sashays were unique to the little railway station in the middle of nowhere.

Almost a year since the Dubber brothers saved up enough to put a down payment on a juke box, and five months since Carson blew the dust off and sent it back, he slapped out the last bits of "Dad" and Dirk announced the next song.

"Ragmuffin Polka."

Everybody cheered.

They were barely into the second verse when two Irish kids walked in. One of them was Mike O'Malley from over at Long Pine. Carson didn't know the other one.

But they both had the right look.

Hard. Tough.

Carson didn't think either one of them would take too much guff.

And he'd heard through the grapevine that Mike O'Malley could probably do the job Carson needed.

The tough job.

Carson picked at the tune, letting Billy take the heavy lead with his bass while he watched Nellie and O'Malley skirt the dance floor to toe the sawdust beside a beer barrel.

The third song was a quartet acapella number by Bill and three fellas from the tent church. Carson took the opportunity to wander over to the beer barrel.

True to the rumor mill, O'Malley wore a gun on his waist.

The kid was tall and wiry. Like an oak tree strung together with long steel cable.

"Mike O'Malley? Mind if I bend your ear a minute?"

O'Malley looked up from his beer and the smile left his face.

"Yes, I do," he said. "And the answer to your offer is no"

"You don't even know what I'm gonna ask you."

"He knows only too well," said O'Malley's friend. "And he ain't gonna do it."

O'Malley grinned at his friend. "Why don't you take a walk? Let me set Mr. Carson straight."

When they were alone, Carson let O'Malley lead him away from the beer barrel into a corner booth under a tin Pepsi-Cola sign. The Irishman had a big pull from his mug and had his say.

"You're asking me to put myself in danger. My wife. My kids."

"Says the man who still carries a sidearm like it was fifty years ago."

"You ain't got a family. Neither does Dirk."

In the background, Bald Billy's colored friends had taken the stage beside him. Dirk tapped his bell and the four began to sing.

Even with as many times as he'd heard it, Carson had to block it out before a lump crawled into his throat.

It was just that beautiful.

And that's what encouraged him to keep pushing O'Malley.

"You should've heard us do 'Dad's Night Out.' Sounded Gadawful." He made a face.

"That bad?"

"Worse."

"Wish I could help you," said O'Malley. "But my fiddle's broke."

"Like hell. They say you had it over to Twosville last week. They say you played for six hours."

"Twosville ain't got no coloreds on stage." O'Malley downed the remainder of his mug, wiping the foam away from his chin with the back of his hand. "If I get up on stage with him, I'm a marked man. Just like you and Dirk."

There it was, laid out straight and simple.

"There's no doubt it's a tough job. But you're a tough man."

O'Malley slid out of the booth and stood

holding his mug beside the sticky pine table.

"I can't handle it the way you can," he said. "You've got a slow temper. You don't mind what people say behind your back."

"I mind plenty. Besides, everybody here loves Billy."

O'Malley's eyes swept the crowd, then landed squarely back on Carson.

"As long as he's singing. As long as he's playing bass. But to be in the same band with him? To be out at night with him? People start thinking low of you."

Carson stood up and faced O'Malley square.

"You're the best fiddle player west of the 98th. I need you in Driftwood. I need you on that stage."

"I ain't so sure what people say isn't true, Carson. That black boy's gotten to you. I think you like playing with ni—"

Before O'Malley could finish the sentence Carson hammered a fist into the bridge of his nose.

The Irishman stumbled backwards, swinging his arm back to right himself, smashing his glass mug into the edge of the booth's high back seat.

Carson closed in quick, shoving O'Malley to the wall and holding him at arm's length like a rattlesnake, his hand a vice-like grip squeezing the Irishman's neck.

"You seem to forget who you're messing with, son. I get up on that stage every night with Bill. Me and Dirk both. We eat with Bill. We spend time at his house. We help his kids with their school." Carson realized his breath was coming fast and hard and everything he said was punctuated with spit landing on O'Malley's face. "Out here, a man's got to be tough. I thought maybe you were tough enough too."

When O'Malley's face started to turn purple, Carson loosened his grip.

"I guess I was wrong about you."

Carson looked around. Nobody had noticed the quick altercation. Or, if they had, they were pretending they hadn't.

On stage, Bill and his friends were wrapping up their number.

Carson's queue to skedaddle.

Without looking back, he turned and headed toward the stage.

Under the hot electric lights, Carson counted time on his guitar, firing into "Steamboat Nancy," while Dirk got his harmonica in place. Bald Billy plunked the bass line on the original tune he wrote specifically for the birth of his third daughter.

Beside him, still wearing a six-gun like it was fifty years ago, Mike O'Malley launched the bow of his fiddle at just the right time to add some jump.

Down the promenade, hands wagged and feet flew.

There were upwards of fifty folks in the barn, and it was way past closing time.

They came to Driftwood with the rail, for the women, for the adventure. They came to Driftwood to prove they were cattlemen, or gunmen, or gamblers.

Some came just to say they'd been there.

Nobody came to make it a home.

As long as Carson's band played, they came for the music.

The Marvelous Brass Penny

Tom Sanderson found Doc Mysterioso's wagon tipped over at the bottom of Toosville Canyon. Tom had a wager going with his neighbor Wes Rackers as to who could shoot the most squirrels in a week's time. Seeing as it was Friday, and seeing as Sunday was the deadline, and Tom was six varmints behind (according to his sister Frieda who spent regular time with Wes), Tom was dang near desperate to find new huntin' grounds. He'd been following a cow trail on the ridge above, straining his eyeballs for any sign of skittering, leaping, squirrel movement when he saw a slash of red far below at the bottom of the valley.

Rather than risk a broken leg or turned hoof on his hoss, Tom left the roan gelding on the path and made his way down the steep embankment, the spicy smell of juniper and jack pine tickling his nose.

Halfway down, Tom lost sight of the red

slash, and he stopped to get his bearings. Tree frogs and trilling cicadas taunted him with noisy glee. With the autumn sun not much past noon they seemed to be out early.

But the trees below were tall enough to make plenty of shadow.

The brome grass he stood on was a yellow green, and clipped short by grazing cattle. He uncorked his canteen, washed his mouth out with water and spit. A black and yellow winged grasshopper rose into the clear sky, leading Tom's eyes to a bunch of black angus cows in the distance. Wes Rackers' new angus herd.

Behind them a string of yellow orange smudges shimmering on the horizon were the buildings of the Sleep Crick settlement.

Up here, close to the Niobrara, close to God, his old man always said, you could see for miles in any direction. You could see the pale white moon, paper thin in the blue heaven above.

You could look down into the dark cedar groves and the burnweed.

Was that a bare, curved tree branch?

Or a wagon wheel?

He capped his canteen and fought gravity to wind his way down, spurred boots firm on the sod incline. Circling east with his decent, it wasn't long before he again saw the red stripe in the brush, recognizing the wreckage.

Resting nearly upside down in a leafy waist-high nest of weeds on the valley floor, its four oak wood wheels high in the air, the scarlet and brass wagon was a bloated dead critter waiting to rot away.

Tom could read part of the legend on the broken hull: Doc Mysterioso. Travel. Medicine. Something else covered in broken vines of creeping jenny.

A nearby trench of upturned earth looked fairly new. And no new growth was visible around the accident. He tried to remember the last time he'd seen or heard about Doc Mysterioso.

It had been a more than a week.

"Hellooo the wagon," Tom called out, pushing through a troublesome stand of Russian Thistles. Tom popped off one of the weeds' purple flowers and balled it up between a leather gloved thumb and forefinger.

He tossed the flower wad at the wreck and it bounced off a broken axel.

A chattering sound came from within and an angry squirrel jumped out and away from the wagon, latched onto a nearby hackberry and climbed out of sight.

Tom kicked himself for leaving his rifle

with the horse.

"Hello? Anybody here?"

That's when Tom realized the cicadas had stopped their trilling.

A feeling, like ants skittering up his neck, made him turn around though he hadn't heard a sound.

Along the flat of the valley, a tall man with a long black duster rode toward him on an open buckboard wagon pulled by two nervous black stallions. The eyes of the horses rolled up and back and Tom could almost count their gnashing teeth. Three additional men rode in the back of the wagon, and the closer they got, the more Tom didn't like their looks.

Two of the men wore only canvas trousers and boots, their naked torsos a darker bronze than any Indian. The third man wore jeans and a paper sack shirt with a brown derby.

All of them were dirty with yellow teeth.

The driver put up his hand in greeting and Tom stayed his ground.

"You want to buy a milk cow?" said the driver.

"How-do," said Tom.

The driver reined in and climbed down from the wagon. He was well over six feet tall and his black duster, pants and tall riding boots made Tom, in his cotton shirt, denim jacket and jeans, feel underdressed.

Hot as it was, the stranger's clean-shaven skin was dry.

Everything about the man was dry. Voice. Manner. Even his eyes were shrunken and gray.

"You didn't answer my question."

"What's that?" said Tom, trying hard to keep his smile friendly.

"You want to buy a cow?"

Tom ran his hand across the stubble on his chin to show polite consideration.

Finally, he shook his head. "Can't say I'm in the market for it."

"Damn shame," said the stranger with more than a hint of frustration. He walked along the side of his buckboard and looked at the three passengers there. "Ain't that a damn shame, boys?"

All three nodded and agreed it was a damn shame.

"You selling cows are you?" said Tom.

"Got me an old milk cow I'd like to lose." The stranger paused, looked at the red wagon wreck as if seeing it for the first time, then he closed one eye and looked at Tom.

"Who the hell are you?"

Cantankerous devil.

Tom had a brother like that. All bluster

and loud talk.

Rather than answer right away, Tom chewed his lip.

"I s'pect I might ask you the same."

"Oh you do? That what you s'pect?"

The stranger didn't seem to be armed. But who could tell what he carried under that long, heavy duster.

And anyway, Tom was outnumbered four to one.

"No offense," said Tom.

"My name's Elias. You got business with this here wagon wreck?" Elias didn't bother to introduce his friends.

"You're not Doc Mysterioso," said Tom.

"No, I'm not." Elias's eyes flicked back and forth from Tom to the men on the buckboard and back. "You know the doc?"

"Maybe."

Only a month or so since Doc Mysterioso pulled into Sleep Crick on a pleasant afternoon not unlike this one. Tom, Wes, and Frieda had been coming out of the mercantile building when the old gent rolled his gaudily painted wagon to a stop in cloud of dust, his voice already booming for attention, his long mane of silver hair shining in the sun.

"You either know him or you don't," said Elias.

"I spent time with him." Tom remembered the jovial old showman's voice, the glint in his eyes, the turquoise Indian beads he wore around his neck.

Tom remembered handing over more money that he should've for various tonics, toys and sugar confectionaries for his sister.

"He was a fine salesman," said Tom.

With a dour face, Elias answered. "He was a magician."

Tom remembered Frieda's glee when Doc pulled an egg from behind Wes's ear.

"Yes he was."

"That wreckage there," said Elias. "That's Satan's work."

"Is it?"

"Who else?" said Elias with a sneer. "Who else would have the power?"

"Plenty of ways to crash a wagon."

Growing up on the high plains, Tom had seen his share of thunderstorms, wind and rain. And to be fair to mother nature, he recalled more than a hint of hooch on Doc's breath.

"What do you know about this wagon, my friend?"

"This here's my property." Elias shrugged. "My land. My wagon."

Tom knew it was a lie, but let it slide. No use picking a lop-sided fight. But still he was curious.

"You know what happened to Doc? How long's this wagon been here?"

"You say you spent time with the doc? Say you know he was a magician?" Elias moved close to Tom and put his hand inside the duster. "I got something for you."

Fear shot through Tom like an electric current, but he didn't have time to react.

Dumbfounded, he stood stock still while Elias pulled a shiny object from an inside pocket and held it out in his palm.

"You take this. It's something I found in that wagon."

"What is it?"

"This here is the marvelous brass penny. Only one like it in the world."

Tom picked up the coin and held it between his thumb and forefinger. It was exactly like any other penny he'd ever seen. On one side, an Indian chief in full feathered headdress. On the other, a buffalo and the legend, "One American Cent."

But the difference was that this penny glowed yellow gold in the sunlight.

Not like copper, but like polished brass.

"That's for you," said Elias.

"I don't understand."

"It's magic. It's got powers. It protects you from bad luck."

"I appreciate it." As he spoke, a movement in the wagon caught Tom's eye. One of the bare chested man now held a rifle. Tom watched as his twin picked up a second gun from the wagon's floor.

"You keep that penny close to you," said Elias. "Bad things been known to happen to folks around here."

Tom wrapped his fingers around the strange coin, held it tight inside a sweaty fist.

"But I wouldn't count on it every time. If you know the Doc, you know how fickle that magic can be."

"I ought to be going now," said Tom. "Got a full afternoon ahead of me."

Elias nodded. "Thanks to that marvelous brass penny, you got a full life ahead of you."

Then he reached up and opened his duster.

Underneath, he wore a collection of turquoise Indian beads around his neck, and at his waist, a leather belt with three long-haired scalps on display.

One of the scalps sported a shiny silver mane.

From a spot less than half a mile back and on the other side of the canyon, Tom sat on his roan with a pair of field glasses and watched Elias and his men pull a heavy steamer trunk from inside Doc Mysterioso's wagon. It took all four men to get the thing up and out of the wrecked hulk.

Before they lifted it into the wagon, Elias shouted something unintelligible and the two shirtless men sat down in the grass beside the trunk. The third man crawled into the wagon and tossed out a hammer. One of the shirtless man started pounding away at the trunk's latch.

When it opened, Tom watched the men paw through the contents.

Clothes. Paper sales bills. Two heavy sacks.

Elias jerked loose the rope tie on one of the sacks and the man with the brown derby reached in to retrieve a handful of gold coins.

Tom grinned to himself.

"Not brass there," he said. "Painted or otherwise."

"What's that, Tom?"

Tom handed the field glasses to Wes Rackers. From the back of his buckskin he took in the view below.

"Looks like they got what they came for," said Wes. "Glad my cows are on the other side of the canyon." He handed the glasses back to Tom who wrapped them up in an oilcloth and put them back into the saddle pack behind him.

"I'm just glad you came around when you did," said Tom. "Hope you don't mind playing deputy."

Carefully, he opened his jacket. Elias wasn't the only one that kept things hidden.

Tom unpinned his marshal's star from his shirt and repositioned it on to the outside of his jacket.

Beside him, Wes checked his rifle. "You ready to go get 'em?"

"Just about," said Tom. From his jacket pocket he pulled the marvelous brass penny.

"What's that?" said Wes.

"Painted brass penny," said Tom. "Doc Mysterioso used to give 'em away for good luck."

"Does it work?"

Tom gazed down on Elias and his boys.

They were completely oblivious to what was coming.

Laughing and shouting at the treasure they'd come back to retrieve, they had no idea how short lived their victory would be.

"Them letting me go. You showing up here when you did."

Tom shoved the coin into his pants pocket. "I'd say the penny works just fine."

Not Much the Cowman

Slumped over in his sheepskin coat on a bed of bug-chewed corn husks in a Nebraska sod cabin, Mike Morris realized it was almost Christmas and he'd missed the fiery Ozarks autumn foliage for the first time in his life. Nothing helped his melancholy, not Slick Peterson's dirty jokes, not Windy Bly's sour smelling mash in the coffee. At the spindle legged cedar table, Slick fumbled with the smoothglass chimney of a kerosene lamp that the wind kept blowing out, while Windy tilted back on the cramped room's only chair, scabby bare knees showing through threadbare holes in his pants.

"Yessirree, things gonna be good for us, boys," said Windy, showing off tobacco stained teeth with a wide grin. Apparently he felt good enough about their future to brag, but Mike held tight to his mope.

"Spring comes and we'll ride through here and take what we want from these dirt farmers," Windy bellowed. "Cows, pigs, maybe even their barefoot, blonde daughters." Ramrod for the owlhoot bunch, Windy always talked like the meanest, most hell-bent rustler around.

Mike jostled his tin cup between two shivering, chapped hands and squinted through sore, dry eyes at the busted window pane with its seemingly endless tendrils of blowing snow.

Things just weren't working out.

Outside, the howling wind carried the mournful bellers of twelve, stolen, scour-plagued Hereford cows they had tucked into this hidey-hole camp east of Sam Catt Trail earlier in the week.

Before the snowstorm hit.

Later, after Windy slapped on his ragged Stetson and lumbered through the thin plank door to go outside and check the cattle, Mike and Slick were alone.

"That frown on your face ain't all about pinin' for home," said Slick. "You been sportin' a bug on for a while now."

Mike held his coat closed. "Reckon after a season of just barely scrapin' by, then bein' socked in here by weather, Windy's got me skeptical about the way things are going."

"Do tell," said Slick, wiping his hands down his greasy trousers. "Damn, it's cold."

Mike continued his lament. "Windy talks about midnight raids and blonde gals, all I see is lawmen and protection committees carrying hemp rope."

"It's winter got you down," said Slick.

"It's Windy and his damn onion breath and you cheatin' at faro."

"Let's just say it's winter."

"I don't like the sky out there, if that's what you mean. Them clouds are achin' to dump another load of snow."

"We got timber to hold out. Horses are fine behind the cabin. Cows got hay and water."

"I wasn't plannin' to hold out," said Mike.

"Well, you know there's a buyer stoppin' around any day now. This fellar Marston gave Windy a $400 down payment. We get paid in full for them beeves, we'll head down to O'Neill City."

"I ain't goin' with you," said Mike. "You maybe didn't understand me."

"You'll think different when you get some cash in hand." Slick pulled out a curling, damp photo pasteboard with a painting of a naked woman on it. "You want to look at my card a while? Cheer you some?"

Mike ignored the offer, but Slick laid the card reverently on the table between them.

"How much you think we're gonna get

for them boney old gals out there?" said Mike. "That's the saddest bunch of cows I ever seen. They was sad when we filched 'em, and they're worse now. And there ain't much hay left. This Marston's gonna want his money back. No sir, I'm through."

"You're gonna quit Windy? You better have your sidearm cocked and ready," said Slick. "He'll lay you out wet and wade right on through."

"That's smoke and you know it. Windy ain't half the hard on he pretends to be." Mike shook his head. "You get right down to it, he just ain't much the outlaw."

"Might be," said Slick. "But he knows cows."

"Like hell. Me, I've worked a ranch or two in my day. So have you. Comes to cattle, you tell me what ol' Windy's got for real life bona fides. Nothing I ever heard about."

"He set up this deal with Marston didn't he? Arranged for the cabin?"

"I didn't say he wasn't good at conniving people. He done roped in you and me."

"He's good with a cow," said Slick.

"Ten dollars says otherwise."

"Ten dollars says what?" Slick got up and poured more coffee.

"Says Windy ain't got what it takes to get them cows through this winter."

"Buyer's comin' any day now," said Slick.

That's when Windy pushed back inside, shivering and slapping at his light wool coat. "Temperature's droppin' boys, and just like I reckoned, that club foot's water broke."

Slick gave Mike a wink, but the Ozarks man just shook his head. He'd hoped the Herefords wouldn't start calving, but sometimes a change in weather hurried such things along.

The next day brought more wind with volleys of thick pasty snow that clung to everything.

"We need to get out and check on the horses," said Mike before noon.

"I stepped out earlier," said Windy. "They're good."

"What about the cows? You make sure the ice broke on the pond so's they all can drink? What about that club foot and her calf?"

"They'll be okay," said Windy. "How about another can of peaches?"

"One can left," said Slick, just crawling up from his blanket. "You want me to open her?"

Mike rubbed his arms. "Ain't nobody gonna fire up the stove?"

"You go ahead," said Slick.

"You ought to make that nudie girl of yours do some of these chores," said Windy. When he laughed, tobacco juice drooled down his chin, but he had his knife out, was cutting a fresh plug.

"My gal's too genteel for that kind of work," said Slick.

"How can a picture be genteel?"

Slick held up the card. "She cost me seven dollars in Vermillion."

Mike brought the furnace up to a healthy burn. "We're about out of wood."

Slick poked the can of peaches with his pocket knife. "Sit down and eat why don't you?"

"Feed it to the cows," said Mike.

"You know somethin', Ozarks?" said Windy. "You're startin' to get on my nerves. This weather's wearin' you out. Sit a spell, won't you?"

Mike looked out the window at the huddled mass of snow-covered cows among the tangled line of trees. He turned back in time to see Windy spear a fat peach with his fork and cram it, dripping, into his mouth.

"Anybody for a round of cards?" said Slick.

"I'm goin' out for that calf," said Mike. "I'll check the pond while I'm at it."

Outside, he didn't mind the wet gobs of

snow but had to continuously close his eyes against the pelting of ice. In an old coat and worn out jeans he wasn't dressed for it. None of them had expected the weather to change so fast.

About two hundred feet, Mike thought, I've walked about two hundred feet from the cabin. But when he turned around all he saw was glaring white and annoying gray blobs that tumbled and fell in his eyes when he stared into the snow. When he turned around again, he'd lost track of the cows.

No buyer was coming in this kind of weather.

Mike didn't know anything about this Marston character, but if he had any sense at all, he'd be far away from northern Nebraska in winter.

Later on, Mike paced around the cabin in red underwear, hanging his frozen wet clothes across the wood backs of chairs to dry, bare feet thawing to pink on the dirt floor.

"Couldn't find the club foot or her calf," said Mike.

Windy took a long swallow of coffee.

"I ever tell you about the winter I spent in St. Louis? Ol' Marston was with me. And he is one mean son." Windy laughed and talked into the night.

■ ■ ■ ■

The next morning, all three men went to look about the cows.

The sun was a blinding wash from a hard, cobalt sky over acres of virgin snow. Piles of white hid entire rows of cedar and made an impasse of the cottonwood shelter that cradled the cabin. The air was bitter cold.

Four of the cows were there, eight were missing.

This time the club foot and her new little heifer weren't more than twenty feet from the stoop. Mike could see the cold had taken its toll because the calf wasn't able to stand.

"I'll go round up them missing eight cows," said Slick, pushing off toward the trees.

"Let's see if we can get this heifer to suck," said Windy, bending down to hoist the babe upright. When it let out a half-hearted bleat, the cow swung around with her head low. Windy stumbled and fell on his butt in the snow.

"Give you a hand," said Mike, but Windy climbed up and pushed him away.

"Never mind that."

The boss man went for the calf again and,

getting it in a tight squeeze, shuffled through the snow aiming straight for the cow's udder. The cow moved, stepping her rear away while keeping eyes pinned on the calf-man staggering sideways toward her. Finally, she turned and took several big steps away toward the huddle of cows in the wood scrub shelter.

Windy was panting hard, his breath chugging like the stack on a steam train. He let the calf drop down into the snow, but stayed doubled over, his raw hands on his knees.

Too bad Slick wasn't there to see it.

Mike had that ten dollar bet in his pocket, sure.

"Let's just forget it," said Windy. "Calf that won't nurse is nature's way of culling the herd."

"You believe that, you're not much the cowman," said Mike.

Windy stepped forward and got close to Mike's face.

"You're so much piss and vinegar, you be my guest," he said. Then, stomping away, "I'm gonna go see if that paper gal of Slick's made us any coffee."

Mike watched the man go into the cabin before turning back to the calf. On the one hand, if he could get the cow roped, maybe tie her to one of the trees, it shouldn't take too much to get some milk into the calf. On the other hand, the newborn didn't have any pep. Might be more important to get her inside, warm her up. One of them could always come out and get some milk in a cup.

Mike had just bent over to carry the calf inside when Slick came back through the trees.

"Bad news, Mike," he said, eyes watering from the cold. "Some branches came down in the storm, knocked out the old fence that was there by the hay."

"The strays?"

"Strays are gone," said Slick. "Wandered off into God knows where."

"Can we fix the fence?"

Slick shook his head. "Ain't no way. That branch is a big, thorny mother."

Mike picked up the calf and turned toward the cabin. "See if you can't rope the club foot and get some milk out of her."

"We got Marston coming any day expecting to pick up some Herefords, and we got four. Four and a half now," he said, nodding at the calf. "Marston don't seem like the sort of man we want to cross. Especially us owing him $400. You heard that story about St. Louis."

"Let me tend to this," said Mike. "You start looking for the cows."

When Mike got inside with the calf, Windy raised holy hell.

"You get that animal out of here," he said. "Ain't nothing to be done for it."

Mike moved the pallet of corn husks close to the stove, wrapped the calf in his and Slick's blankets and rubbed it all over. The calf shook like jelly, her tongue half out of her mouth.

"Slick's gonna rope the clubfoot. Try to get some milk."

"You check on the herd?" asked Windy.

Mike shrugged, and didn't tell him about the missing cows.

Before too long, Slick came in for a cup, went out, and came back with it two thirds full of fresh milk. When he handed it over to Mike, he made the slightest negative move with his head.

He wasn't able to find the strays.

Gently, the two men tried to get some nourishment into the calf while Windy paced around and slurped coffee. When the boss started spinning the chamber of his Colt, Mike squared off against him in the corner.

"You don't have to like it, but we're savin' that calf."

"You done what you could. Take it back outside now," said Windy.

"If a man's gonna live off cattle, even behind the law, a man ought to care a little bit about 'em," said Mike.

"Why think so?"

Mike spread his empty hands. "It just seems like the way it should be."

"You and Slick know cows. I know money. Cows mean money. So here we are." Windy waved the pistol high. "Beyond that, I couldn't care."

"Sell me the club foot and the calf," said Mike.

"What?"

"Sell them to me. You say you don't want 'em. Marston ain't gonna want 'em."

Mike held Windy's look. He thought he could almost see the decision being weighed.

He didn't pay any attention to the gun.

"Alright, I'll write you up a bill of sale."

"How much you want?" said Mike.

"Everything I paid you for this job so far."

Mike dug in his pocket, pulled out a roll of bills.

"Done," he said, slamming it onto the table.

"Let's get that calf back outside," said Mike over his shoulder. "Check on the rest of the herd. And Slick? How about we take our canteens over to the pond and fill up with some fresh water?"

"Now you're thinking straight," said Windy. "Take mine too."

Windy laid his gun on the table, wrote the bill of sale on the back of Slick's girlie card.

After Mike signed it, Windy smiled. "When you boys get back in, I'll tell you about the time Marston and me hoo-rahed a Wyoming tent town."

"Now who's down in the dumps?" said Mike as they rode through the cedars, down from the high country, away from Windy and the cabin, cutting a straight path toward the Elkhorn river. The snow wasn't piled as high here, but Mike still held fast to the rope that led the club foot. On his left, Slick had the calf wrapped in the two blankets.

"Aw, it's just that I paid seven dollars for that painted girl. Now she's yours."

Mike made a show of doing the math in the air.

"Way I see it," he said, "you owe me ten dollars for our bet about Windy. I'll give you seven for the girl. You still owe me three."

Mike felt his legs involuntarily clench the saddle when he saw the dark rider come around a bend on the trail ahead of them.

Mike and Slick drew their horses to a stop.

The rider wore a heavy black coat over thick wool clothes and a brown fleece wool wrap around his throat. Big ivory handled pistols waited in black holsters at his belt. A scar ran up his cheek through one dead eye.

"Afternoon," he said. "My name's Marston. Looks like you got caught in the snow."

Mike cleared his throat. "Sure as hell," he said. "Club foot here wandered off to have her calf in a drift."

"Cow's always gotta wander off to calf," said Marston.

"Are you a cow man, Mr. Marston?" said Mike.

"That I am."

Mike thought about Windy back at the cabin. By now he'd be wondering how long his boys were going to stay out. He might even step outside to look for them.

There was a slim chance he'd venture as far as the broken fence and realize the cows were gone.

Mike appraised Marston once more, then smiled at the grim hard case scalper who carried twin Colts.

How would he react to riding all the way up here for nothing?

"I reckon we better ride on," said Mike.

"You get that calf inside tonight," said Marston.

"Will do."

They rode a while in silence. After a few miles, Slick said, "You're a good cowman, Mike. But I think you still got some outlaw in you. I don't think you ought let that go."

"Aw, Slick."

"Now don't 'Aw, Slick' me. You just listen to what I been thinkin' about."

And visiting natural like while the cow followed, they headed toward O'Neill City.

The Consulting Detective of Darbyville

Maestro Vale leaned back, propping his patent leather shoes up on the sheriff's oak desk, then laced his fingers flat across the small ball of his stomach. He wore a brown corduroy vest and suit coat over a long-sleeved yellow shirt. He smelled of bay rum cologne.

Sheriff Cheyenne Ned wore a short sleeved cotton shirt, didn't smell half as good, and sweated out a pint sitting down.

The law office window was open to the clip-clopping of horses and the squeak of dusty wagon wheels. In the distance, the continuous hammering of new construction.

With the railroad coming in less than a year, Darbyville's star was on the rise.

Vale was cool as a cucumber, and the dude's stomach reminded Ned of a cantaloupe. Matter of fact, to Ned, Vale seemed a little fresh out of the garden. Couldn't be more'n nineteen or twenty years old.

Ned figured he was already breaking a wild horse or taming a town of drunken punchers the first night Vale drew breath. Now here was Vale, hired by the founder as some kind of detective consultant.

"Sheriff, what are the biggest problems this town's got?" Vale spread his hands apart and opened his fingers wide. "I mean the biggest. Give it to me straight."

Ned scratched his head.

"Well, I got old man Childress selling green meat down at the Exchange. I've warned him time and again."

"Green meat. Check. What else?"

"Mrs. O'Connor's turned her daughter out for nightly visits at the Café." Ned shook his head. "Sure is stirring up the pimple faced boys."

"Green meat. Green men. Check. What else?"

"What else is there?"

"What if I told you I could make this place a paradise on Earth? Quiet nights. Quiet weekends. No crime?"

"Pretty quiet as it is."

"You call that quiet?" said Vale, swinging his hand back toward the hammering at the future railroad yard.

"I call it progress."

"You don't worry that some of those roughnecks on the line down there will come into town tonight and tear things up?"

"Most of them roughnecks grew up around here. Besides, we keep a pretty close eye on 'em."

"Close enough to know the future?"

"What are you aiming at, Mr. Vale? The Mayor and Justice Smith said I got to listen to your spiel. They didn't say for how long."

"I can tell you who's going to commit a crime, as well as the specifics of that crime before it happens."

"How so?"

"With this." Vale put his feet flat on the wooden floor and reached for his valise. Standing, he swung it up under the sheriff's nose and opened it. Ned peered down at the strange looking piece of pine that had letters and numbers burned into it while Vale produced a narrow champagne glass. He turned the glass upside down and put it on the center of the board.

"The Ouija can see the future."

"I'll be dogged," said Ned.

"Put your fingers on the stem of the glass. Please don't push or otherwise try to influence its movement. Just follow it around the board."

Vale put his fingers on the foot of the glass

opposite Ned.

"Ouija," said Vale in a commanding tone. "Who is in the room with me."

Slow and smooth, the glass slid around the board, stopping first at N, then E, then ending up at the letter D.

"That's darned impressive," said Ned.

"And to prove its acumen in predicting crime, I took the liberty of asking it two questions before our interview. First, I asked about any shady business deals going on in town."

"What'd the board tell you?"

Vale produced a slip of paper. On it was written, "Meetings."

Ned looked up blankly. "Meetings?"

Vale shook his head vigorously. "Meat, meetings. Meetings, meat. You said you were having a problem with green meat."

Ned stroked his three day growth of stubble. "That's kind of a stretch."

"Good lawmen have to stretch."

"What about the other one?"

Vale handed over the paper.

"Girl," said Ned. "That's it?"

"That's enough. It gives you the first thing to go on."

"I see, I see." Ned slid the Ouija board away and leaned across the desk. "And how much did you say you were charging the town for your consulting services?"

"Why, er . . . only two hundred."

"Dollars?"

"Um. Yes."

"But it's ultimately up to me to hire you or not?"

"Naturally," said Vale. "Naturally."

They sat quietly for a few minutes while the sheriff leaned back and thought about Maestro Vale and his Ouija board.

Finally, the pounding of hooves signaled the arrival of Deputy Jim.

Ned walked to the window and brushed aside one of the curtains.

"Here we are," he said. "I think now you'll have your answer."

"I don't understand," said Vale.

The office door opened for Ned's deputy, shoving ahead of him a bespectacled young man wearing a suit nearly identical to Vale's. In fact, nearly every feature, from his hair to his nose to his melon round stomach was identical with Vale.

"Jerry Stump," said Deputy Jim. "Found him just where you figured, camping outside town on the other side of the railbed."

"Jerry Stump," said Ned. He looked at Vale. "That would make you Billy Stump then, wouldn't it? Your name ain't Vale at all." The sheriff nodded at Jim. "The Stump

Brothers are wanted all across Nebraska for assorted confidence tricks and falsified claims. Good work, Jim."

Vale shook his head. "That's fine detective work, Sheriff. But I can't see how you could've known. How'd you know to send out your deputy for my brother?"

Cheyenne Ned smiled a toothy grin. "Mrs. O'Connor?"

At the invitation, a young girl with long black braids dressed in a flowing silk blouse and pantaloons with a blue sash appeared from an adjacent room.

"You're Mrs. O'Connor?" said Vale.

Ned nodded. "Deputy Jim O'Connor's wife."

"But what does she have to do with anything?"

The Sheriff opened a drawer on his desk and pulled out a big, oversized card.

He flipped it across the desk where it landed face up in front of Vale.

The Twins.

"A . . . a tarot card? Like . . . like gypsies use?"

"The founders hired Mrs. O'Connor last year," explained the sheriff. "It's how she and Jim met."

Ned chuckled as Jim led the twins toward a corner jail cell.

"Mrs. O'Connor is sort of a . . . consulting detective."

The Oddsmakers

Here's something straight from a melodrama, thought the gambler Eddie Drake as he watched the fat man, Anderson Salich, kick up the dust and bawl like a mad cow.

Lounging on the hotel bench in a black claw-hammer coat, flipping his pocket watch open and shut, Drake pretended not to be interested.

"My heart cries vengeance," called Salich, swinging his left arm into a great arc that braked with an accusing finger sending a flicker of sweat toward one of the cowboys on the boardwalk.

Yessir, thought Drake, Salich is a second-rate actor, but a first rate romantic.

Just past noon, and Salich was working his ass off.

Drake tilted back his black hat to brush aside a lock of long, iron red hair.

You usually didn't get entertainment like this so early in the day.

"The man sounds like a circus barker," said a thin man in leather chaps who leaned over a hitching rail two steps from Drake.

"Or a preacher," said skinny's bearded friend.

Sweating and red faced, dressed nice enough to be the latter, loud enough to be the former, Salich called the townsfolk to attention.

"You cattle men of Valentine are scoundrels," he said with vulgar glee. "Creeping philanderers."

A hapless little drover standing in front of a store clawed at his neckerchief and chewed the corner of his untrimmed black and silver mustache.

Even from across the sunbaked street, Drake saw the unarmed man tremble.

"I will have my reckoning," said Salich, swiping a woolen suit coat sleeve over his shining bald head.

Reckoning. There was a good two dollar word.

Hand polished and warm in Drake's palm, the pocket watch clicked open and shut and a breeze picked up a scent of garlic chicken and buttery potatoes from inside the hotel.

The skinny man launched a stream of rancid black tobacco into the street. "This won't end well," he said.

Beside him, the bearded cowboy rolled a smoke and nodded in agreement. "Here comes the law," he said.

Stepping out of the hotel, Constable Bob Bailey belched and hitched his thumbs behind a worn leather belt.

"Friend of yours?" said Bailey, a smile in his gray slate eyes.

"Never seen 'im before," said Drake.

Bailey nodded. "Me neither. But I know the type."

He pulled up his britches by the belt, then let his right palm fall on the butt of a holstered Army Colt .45.

"You ain't gonna need that," said Drake.

Bailey squinted into the street, then peered down at Drake.

"I beg to differ. See where his coat jacket flares out? The man's carrying a gun in a shoulder rig."

"I just don't think he'll use it." Drake shrugged. "Ten dollars says he won't use it."

"And if he does and I come out on the wrong end?"

"I'll raise a glass in your honor and put ten towards your funeral expenses."

Bailey grinned. "I'll take that."

Then he stepped off the boardwalk, the tin star on his long sleeved flannel shirt gleaming in the sun.

Salich's full attention was on the little boardwalk cowboy. "I do believe you're the man soiled my wife," he said. "My wife!"

"That's enough outta ya," said Bob Bailey.

Salich turned and addressed the constable. "You would defend this monster?"

Drake almost laughed out loud.

The little drover weighed less than 100 pounds and was draped in a blue cotton shirt with saggy brown pants.

A monster.

Priceless.

"Who wants to make a bet, boys?" said Drake, loud enough for two of the nearby cowboys to hear.

Drake watched the constable stop three feet away from Salich and played through the numbers in his head.

Odds were rock solid against peaceful old Bailey drawing first on a man.

But you never knew for sure.

After all, there was indeed a shoulder rig under Salich's coat.

Not knowing.

That's where the fun came in.

"What's your bet?" said the thin man.

"I'll wager Constable Bailey takes the man's gun and brings him in peaceably," said Drake.

■ ■ ■ ■

In the street, the scene continued to play out like an opera house number.

"Care to explain yourself, mister?" said Bailey.

"I'm not the wronged party here, sir."

"I'll be the judge of that. What's your name?"

"Salich. Anderson Salich."

"Well, Mr. Salich if you have a complaint against one of the men here, maybe we should take it to my office." The constable spread his arms apart. "Away from the women and children."

Salich stepped back to widen his stance.

That there weren't any women or children for three blocks around didn't seem to matter to Bailey, but Drake saw Salich turn a deeper shade of red.

"As I stated, I'm not the wronged party."

The skinny man turned to Drake. "Bet you a dollar Bailey has to kill him."

The bearded cowboy nodded. "At least they'll go to fisticuffs. Two dollars."

"Are we children?" said Drake. "Let's be sporting."

The cowboys both raised their eyebrows.

"Ten," said Drake.

"Too rich for me."

In the street, Salich's furrowed brow shadowed red, fury-filled eyes.

"I will make my stand here," he said.

The wind became a breeze and the breeze trickled away to a whispering breath.

Bailey put his hand flat on the butt of his gun.

Nobody else moved and the dust lay dead and reddening in oncoming afternoon shadow.

"On second thought, okay, ten," said the skinny man.

"I'm in," said the beard.

"I'll tell you once more, Mr. Salich," said Bailey. "Come with me to the office."

Salich licked his lips, moved his eyes back and forth.

Drake gave a slight nod.

"All right. All right, I'll come with you," said Salich. "I don't want no trouble. Not really."

"Hand over your weapon," said Bailey.

Salich seemed to consider the request, looked around at his audience. "Not that I don't trust you, but . . . ," Finally, he waved his right hand at Drake. "How about I turn it over to that man there? He looks like a good egg."

Bailey laughed. "Now I know you're

drunk, Mr. Salich. But it's fine with me."

When the two men stepped up to the boardwalk, Drake was on his feet, collecting his winnings from the two cowboys.

Salich handed him his gun.

"Looks like I owe you something too," said Bailey.

"Let's settle up inside."

Through the hotel door and to the right, the constable's office was flooded with sunlight.

Behind a closed door, Drake and Salich sat on stools before a big oak desk.

After a few minutes, Bob Bailey came in, locked the door behind him, and poured three tumblers of blazing amber Scotch.

He passed out the drinks, then tossed a roll of ones and fives into the center of the desk.

"That's from the lunch crowd. Before I came out. Odds were three to one I'd blow your head off."

Drake added his twenty. "From the boys on the boardwalk."

Bailey divided the take equally between them.

It wasn't as much as Drake had taken in Chadron, but it was okay.

Salich pocketed his share with a flourish.

Happy enough.

Finishing his drink, Bailey said. "You boys best slip out of town the back way. Your horses are waiting behind the hotel."

"And the sheriff in O'Neill knows we're coming?"

"Yes indeed. Talked to him about it the other day. He's betting on you."

"He'd be a fool not to," said Salich. "I'm the best actor west of the Missouri."

Then he stood and wiped his head on the sleeve of his coat.

"Shall we go?"

Drake nodded, shook the constable's hand.

"Pleasure doing business with you, Bob."

"Come back anytime."

"You can bet on it," said Drake.

A Change of Plans

"Kid's gang will take the stage below," said Sheriff Mark Walters. "You shoot the Kid. I'll cover you."

Earl got into position. A crack shot, the best Mark could find on short notice.

"How will I know him?

"Always wears a red shirt," said Mark.

Earl nodded.

"No prettier country than these Flint Hills of Kansas," said Mark, gazing across the emerald field.

"I'm color blind," said Earl. "It's all brownish grey to me."

Mark scratched his chin.

The stage appeared on the horizon.

"Tell you what," said Mark. "I'll take out the Kid, you cover the gang."

The Worst That Could Happen

Overlooking Hellstone settlement in the full moonlight, Jug Calamity sat tense in the saddle, one hand on the horn, one hand nervously scratching the black stallions' withers, considering the prospect below him.

"One of them ol' miners down there finally hit the mother lode day 'fore yesterday," said Stink Fallon from the cedar brush on Jug's left.

"They say there's enough gold dug out already to put you in a sweet pot the rest o' forever," said Willy Bass, standing with his horse on the bare granite at right.

Happy conversation and light fiddle music came from the huddled group of poorly lit tents and stacked wood structures below. Jug could smell the miners' warm bacon and beans, could almost taste the celebratory whiskey he knew would be flowing. He snorted. Hellstone couldn't have a population more than fifty. Well fed and drunk.

Stink tapped the Colt .45 on his hip. "Let's take this town," he said.

"Old miners, half dozen Chinese cooks. This will be no trouble," said Willy. Jug watched Willy pull the cigarette from his mouth and blow the ember red hot. "Want me to burn 'em out, Boss?"

Jug pursed his lips with indecision.

"Hell, what's the worst that could happen?" said Stink.

That's just what was eatin' Jug.

The worst that could happen.

"Let's say we do it Willy's way," said Jug. "Let's say we get a good burn going. Maybe take out these tents over here." He spread his arm to the north. "Wind's picking up some and will carry to the shacks over yonder."

"Exactly my thoughts," said Willy.

Jug cleared his throat. "Meantime, we pound thunder, come in from that ridge above the music. Over there." He pointed and saw Stink nod with a smirk.

"Wherever there's most people, that's where they'll have the gold too."

Jug knew it too. And he knew this time they'd get what they were after.

Six months on the prod with Stink and Willy, dodging the law and scraping sand at every turn. Now it was all down to one fast, bloody job. Then Jug could retire. Even a fraction of the gold Hellstone was rumored to have would keep him in the sauce for years.

Jug could finally go home.

Back to Mississippi. Back to Verna Mae.

After the war, and wounded in the hip, he'd followed dark trails into the west. Of course, his name wasn't really Jug Calamity, that's just what everybody called Jake Callahan once he earned a reputation.

"You know boys," said Jug with a hint of melancholy in his voice, "this last several months hasn't paid off all that well."

"This time is different though, right Boss?"

Jug gave Willy a wink. "I'm saying it is," said Jug.

This time would absolutely pay off.

Once they got all the gold they could carry into their saddle bags, Jug would put a bullet or three into Stink and Willy quick as spit and take the three horses back east. At some point he'd change the gold to currency and lose two of the horses.

Or maybe he'd bring the horses along home. Verna Mae would love the sorrel gelding Willy rode. He imagined her pampering the horse with endless brushing and extra molasses in his feed.

He imagined Verna might pamper him a little too.

Not that he'd make her cook or wait on him. They'd have servants for that.

When they weren't out strolling through the city.

His brow furrowed at the picture in his head. He'd have to get a jewel encrusted cane to relieve some of the pain of his hip.

And why not a fine collection of silk trousers with colorful braces and a gold pocket watch?

Even though silk always made his crotch chafe.

But hell, it didn't matter what he wore. Verna would be with him. They'd have everything they wanted.

Or she would, he thought.

"What a man might do with all that gold, eh Stink?" said Willy, lighting a fresh smoke.

Jug listened and clenched his teeth.

He might take up horses.

But he really didn't like horses, mostly because they didn't like him.

Maybe he'd invest in real estate. Just sit back with Verna and watch the nest egg grow.

Maybe plant a garden.

He could collect stamps.

Or taste fine wines.

No, he thought, his stomach wouldn't take that.

And all the time, Verna would be on his arm, chattering away. Her voice, endless as the wind, and shrill like a late-season blizzard. And before long, a passel of bratty kids.

"I think I'll check into a fine hotel somewhere," said Stink. "Sleep until noon. Get up, let some fresh young thing feed me lunch, then take a long nap until supper."

"Sounds like heaven," said Willy.

"Sounds like the grave," said Jug. "Laying around. Sleeping."

"I wouldn't be sleeping at night," said Stink. "If you get my meaning, boss."

"And you'd pay for that too, wouldn't you?" said Jug. "Dying a little more each day."

He shook his head, shook it hard to clear it all away, the jewels and the silks and the servants.

Slow poison!

It was the worst that could happen, and it was a hair's breadth away, as close as a stray spark off Willy's smoke.

Jug practically fell from his saddle, snatching the cigarette from Willy's mouth with a gloved hand.

"Put that out," he said. "Let's get the hell out of here."

"But Jug," said Willy, "What about Hellstone?"

Jug shook his head and led them away from the settlement. Once they were back on the open range, he felt relief wash over him.

The boys didn't know it, but they'd dodged a bullet with this one.

"Hellstone, Jug?"

"No boys," he said as he led them toward the dark horizon, "the price was just too damned high."

West of Noah

According to the Indians, Coyote is the trickster.

He can change shapes, appear in two places at once, and sometimes — when the stars align just right — become invisible.

When Hobnail Higgins found scat on a trail west of Noah, he forgot all the wild stories. He only had one thing in mind.

He was hellbent to blast a brush wolf.

That anything other than an honest-to-St. Pete coyote had dropped the drying turds never crossed his mind.

Thirteen years-old, Hob had never been hoodwinked before.

He turned his back on the scat, and the great hunter was off for the far reaches of the trail.

Hob wanted a coyote more than anything in the world. Not for the pelt or because the dogs had become a nuisance to the community, but just to show Dowd Dempsey and Stick McCain and the Kempker boys that he was good as any of 'em when it came to guns, guts, and gumption.

West of Noah, the vast pan of Wyoming grass was still and the morning sky a lid of gray dark clouds, and Hob had marched away from Ma's one-room cabin in the Laramie foothills without bothering to bring along lunch or a jug full of water.

He lugged his pa's Henry .44 up against his shoulder, like a soldier, proud and erect. After a while, he got tired and cradled it in his arms, tender — like a newborn calf. The durned thing wasn't so much heavy as awkward, and since sunrise he'd come a good four miles from home.

He'd been looking forward to this day — his thirteenth birthday — for a long time.

Ever since Ma laid down the date he could go out and hunt alone — all by himself.

He'd been waiting ever since his pa died in bed, shriveled up in the parlor room, a few last words of instruction on his lips. "Hobnail, make good now," he said. "You make good."

I will, Papa.

From somewhere up ahead there came a mournful wail. Wiping each hand in turn on the slick worn thighs of his loose corduroy britches, Hob reclaimed his manly grip on the rifle's hard steel barrel.

Hobnail Higgins surged forward.

The first week of October had accommodated Hob with an opening volley of overcast days and afternoon rain that caught the local aspens dropping their leaves like tongues of dying embers to the cold grass.

Days where the air was wet and perfectly attuned to the coyote's frenzied cries.

Hob listened to them from his bedroom window each night before sleep, anticipating his big hunt. On the eve of his birthday, he'd gone to bed with the daylight, and sirens of the brush wolf pack called to him from the dark with a scurrilous nature that made two or three seem like ten.

Coyote — the trickster.

Far enough across the range for Hob to feel brave.

In his imagination there were dozens of the ornery devils, maybe hundreds, and he saw himself standing triumphant on a pile of bloody pelts, the head of the biggest king coyote held high in both hands. Dowd, and Stick, and the Kempker boys crouching far below.

Surrounding him on all sides of the mountain, the girls from school looked up to him with admiration.

The cowboys and church ladies smiled

with respect.

In the morning, Hob left a hasty note for his ma, and set out along Japheth Crick for the open range past Ketchum's place.

Ketchum trapped all sorts of game — coyote included — but the crazy old coot never showed himself in Noah. Some folks said he hadn't been to town in forty years. Sniffing the sage October air, Hob felt a drop of water hit his nose even as his stomach complained for the twentieth time.

Hob told his stomach to pipe down.

He could always pop a squirrel or rabbit later on.

Ketchum's land was stuffed with game.

First would come the brush wolf.

To his left was Japheth creek, running high with brown water and rimmed with a scarf of cedar trees and chaff bent low and covered in mud from recent floods. The land to his right was an open swale — a vast expanse of gamma grass, bowing away from him, stunted and yellow all the way to the horizon. He imagined the coyote bounding out over the prairie, haughty and full of vinegar, the animal's tarnished dark coat ruffled by its passage, its ears pricked high, nose twitching, eyes sharp as a hawk.

It would be completely ignorant of Hob and the Henry firm against his shoulder.

Hob pulled the rifle up and, not wanting to waste a cartridge, pretended to lob a round at the imaginary beast without pulling the trigger.

The iron sites were clear under his lashes.

His breath came easy as he turned in harmony with his make believe target.

Hob imagined squeezing the trigger, oh so gentle now . . . slowly letting out his breath . . .

There would be a loud explosion.

A blanket of starlings would lift high above the creek from their nests.

Under the weight of Hob's bullet, the brush wolf would roll and twist, kicking up a cloud of dirt. Hob would have to fire once, twice, maybe three more times to take down such a monster.

"Ker-schpoooooow," whispered Hob.

It was going to be glorious.

A few hundred yards off the trail, blocking off the fields beyond, the tall rocky butte that King Ketchum used as a property line and fence reared up like an ancient castle fortress. Hob followed its black granite rim for half a mile along the horizon, wondering how much property Ketchum owned. Off in the distance, he heard the strained howl he'd heard before, and his fingers tightened on the rifle stock.

It could have been a coyote. It must have been.

A hedge of multiflora rose bush stood up from the crick bank and covered the base of the imposing rocky butte like a thorny apron — the perfect place for a critter to nest. A safe place for a coyote's den of pups.

Maybe?

Fueled by fantasy, Hob left the path and trudged toward the tall rock outcropping, his tongue rough against dry lips, his stomach scraping his backbone.

As soon as he bagged the coyote, he'd find some game. Maybe build a fire.

The air smelled heavy with rain from the north and . . . a wild odor Hob's couldn't place.

He lifted his chin and his toe hit something hard and he wind milled forward, almost losing the rifle, almost eating the dirt. What the heck had he tripped over?

Buried in a soft red clay, the old sign came loose in two pieces, a knobby cedar pole and a roughhewn plank with words sunfaded and barely legible. Hobs picked up the sign and read it.

No trespassing.

Hob let the board fall back at his feet and carried on.

If King Ketchum had a problem with him being there, then old King Ketchum could just come down from his high palace on the other side of the bluff and stop him.

Hob bit his lip and screwed up his nerve. "Just let him try to stop me," he said.

Tossing the Henry back on his shoulder, he marched ahead, full of defiance. The clouds played along, grumbling under their breath with thunder.

More sprinkles. And then the rain came down, reluctant spatters at first, dollops of cold water slapping at Hob's thin linsey shirt. Then an even, steady fall.

Hob mopped water from his eyes.

How long, he thought, before he turned around? How long until he gave up?

After all, he had plenty of time to make it back home before supper. He imagined Ma's table with a blue gingham cloth lousy with taters and gravy and a platter stacked with ham. Bowls of bread stuffing and a hot pie cooling on the stove. Hot lemon tea.

This time the howl came with a warning growl after, and Hob knew it was a coyote.

He was sure of it.

There, shadowed against the wall of the butte, where the flat grass was washed away and the range was speckled with a few prickly pears, an animal swayed back and forth on four legs. Hob picked out the shape against the background rock.

The beast gave off a series of staccato yips punctuated by enraged yowls.

It didn't look like a coyote.

Transfixed, Hob walked toward the creature.

Too big to be a coyote. A wolf? For a wild split-second Hob imagined it was a moose.

Impossible, thought Hob. There hadn't been a moose around Noah for a coon's age. At least, that's what Ma said.

The rain came hard and the sweep of it soaked down Hob's clothes and blurred his vision.

He hunched over the gun with an impossible idea of keeping it dry. But he kept moving forward, confident because of his weapon, lured toward the curious figure at the bluff, a dark shape now pacing in a tight circle.

He walked from a clear space of mud into a patch of grass less than a hundred yards away and the curtains of rain parted. Hob held the rifle up, muzzle pointed at the sky with one hand while he knuckled water from his vision.

In front of him, the creature growled low in its throat, with an odd whistle, like a dying steam engine.

Or one just getting started.

Hob's loose, rolling stomach pulled tight with a near-painful tug. His feet were iron weights sinking into the clay.

He was closer than he'd imagined. Less than thirty feet.

The black bear curled back his top lip and bared his yellow-brown fangs.

It was a healthy young male, not yet fully grown, but rippling with life. This was no mangy, rail-thin scavenger.

No, this was a trophy, a sleek monarch with thick black fur who reared up on two legs shoulder high and weighed twice as much as Hob, and maybe then some again.

With pitched ears and clear eyes, the beast rocked up and down, seemingly set to pounce.

Hob felt a flutter in his chest travel up both arms like an electric shock and his hands fumbled around with the rifle.

He dropped it just as the bear made its move.

Hob toppled backwards onto his behind, rolled, made a sprawling grab for the rifle —

Felt a thud vibrate through his wrist, then saw only red as a searing jolt of agony tore through his arm. For an instant, that's all there was to Hob's world — pain and sheets of red followed by an all-enveloping darkness.

Hob couldn't move, could only scream out loud, the noise pouring out of him like a torrent.

Then he jerked open his eyes and saw the horrible truth.

His wrist was broken, crushed in the horrible steel jaws of a fur-trader's trap, the iron vice staked with a chain to a patch of bare earth.

Hob struggled to catch up to the pain. Struggled to control his breathing.

King Ketchum had stopped him after all.

Then the bear wailed — like an eerie mix of a heavy dog's bark and a Tom cat's squealing cry. But not exactly like either, and Hob flipped over to his back, tearing at the skin of his mangled wrist, enduring the torment to kick with his heels away from the lunging, snapping jaws of the creature.

"Grawrf, rarf, raaaar!"

The bear kept its distance.

Hob rolled back, frantically circling the stake in the ground, dragging out the attached chain with his captured wrist at the end to its farthest possible length. He saw the Henry .44 resting in the saturated grass and stretched out his good arm.

A foot too short.

He cried with frustration and pain, pounding the ground, the bear's insistent growls punctuating a rolling squall of thunder overhead, his hulking shadow lunging . . .

But it never reached Hob.

At the last second, the bear yelped and shied away, and the clouds cut loose with an ocean.

Hob rolled onto his stomach and struggled to slow down his breathing.

The bear was gone.

Why? How?

Madly, Hob decided maybe it had seen the gun. Maybe somebody had taken a few shots at it once or twice before and it had learned to fear the firestick.

Firestick — like the Indians in books called a rifle.

Indians called coyote the trickster.

Was that it?

Hob had ventured out to hunt a coyote. Was this him — the trickster, the shape-changer in the form of a bear?

Or was bear a trickster as well?

Was this momentary reprieve a prank? Was the bear waiting for him to open his eyes? To sit up? Would it come for him at any second with wild eyes and gaping jaws?

Hob listened to the roar of the rain, felt it trickling down his face.

The iron bite of Ketchum's trap was excruciating but he thought he could move without crying.

Slowly, he lifted himself up on his left arm and then into a sitting position before his heart stopped once again.

The bear also sat. Six feet away.

Staring at him with bare teeth.

Drenched, miserable in the storm, the bear lips twitched and the slow growl from his chest continued, like the rumble of an interior grindstone spinning . . . ever spinning.

Hob sat stock still, let his eyes play over the scene.

It had to be a trick. Maybe the bear was sick with rabies. Playing with him before racing forward to tear out his throat.

The bear didn't look sick. His eyes were clear.

He looked scared.

Probably the same way Hobnail looked to the bear.

"Hey, boy . . . ," he ventured. "Hey —"

The beast lurched forward with a mad yapping and Hob flinched. But this time he kept his eyes open and watched with amazement as — mid-leap — the attack was cut short. The bear fell backwards. Once again it cried out with pained frustration.

Then Hob saw it, the bloody bare spot where the iron clamp had rubbed away the fur, heard the rattle of the chain as the animal fell back to nip at his right back leg.

Another one of King Ketchum's traps.

The two of them were in the same pickle then.

Trapped by a set of iron jaws affixed at the hinge to a chain two feet-long, the chain in turned attached to a steel stake driven into the ground. Hob was caught at the wrist. The bear, in his trap, was held by his back leg. Each of them claimed a circle of territory around his central stake.

The circles intersected, but as long as Hob stayed on the far side of his stake from the bear, chain stretched to its full length, he was out of reach.

The bear couldn't hurt him.

As long as Hob's stake held, he couldn't reach the rifle.

He was no threat to the bear.

"I won't hurt you, boy," said Hob, trying to block out his morning's dreams of doing far more than that to a coyote or dinner-time rabbit. Even now, soaked to the skin, with a broken wrist, he couldn't help but think what a prize the bear's hide would make.

For his part, the bear turned away from

Hob. He was complacent now, sitting at the far edge of his circle, panting, letting the rain pour over his broad forehead without blinking, occasionally lashing his narrow snout with a long pink tongue.

But there was no way to know how long Sam was going to behave.

Sam. As good a name as any for a bear.

Hob's wrist was throbbing and purple but the bleeding had stopped. Any attempt to pry open the trap with his free hand resulted in shards of pain that made his head swim.

Instead of getting free, he tried capturing the gun — two tasks equally impossible.

Even stretched out flat in the mud, he couldn't reach it — not even with the toe of his boot.

At one point, Sam wandered over into Hob's territory. Inside the circumference of the trap's circle, the bear swatted at the stake that held Hob's chain.

"You trying to help me, boy?" Hob marveled at the look of curiosity on the bear's face. "Or are you asking for help?"

Sam peeled back his jowls, snuffed and wheezed a half-hearted answer before backing away into his own place.

Another wave of rain came, and when Sam finally settled down again, Hob used his good hand to dig at the trap's deeply embedded stake. It must've been at least two feet long, driven to the earth tight with a hammer.

Hob sat back, the nails of his fingers caked with loam.

He wished he had the bear's claws. He jerked his head to the right and, spying the other trap's stake saw that yes — Sam had been digging at his anchor too. For all the good it had done him. The bear's stake was just as firm as Hob's.

Maybe he had been asking Hob for help after all.

Fatigue washed over him with the storm, and this time the rain didn't stop.

Late in the afternoon, Sam acted out again, scuffled around, dug some more at his stake with his forepaws, then thrust his claws through the hinged steel locked around his back foot. He whimpered and cajoled, roared with rage and shook himself into a frenzy.

Hob stayed at the far end of his leash, wondering what would happen if Sam got free. Would the bear rend Hob from chin to chuckwagon?

Or would he run loose in the opposite direction?

Hob didn't want to find out, so he stayed as vigilante as he could against the increasing cold.

Unable to control the trembling.

The day wore on and the rain didn't end. Puddles appeared on the open range. Puddles that became ponds.

Ponds threatening to grow into lakes.

Hob's empty stomach was a chronic ache, his arm a numb, dead weight. Before long, he couldn't keep his eyes open.

When he woke up, it was dusk. He had to relieve himself something awful, but was ashamed to wet his pants.

Laying in a shallow pool of rain slop, soaked to the skin like a sponge in a hog wallow, he couldn't help but wonder what difference more water could make?

Afterwards, he felt better and rolled onto his back with mouth agape, slurping at the fresh water from the sky. As long as the clouds kept giving, he wouldn't die of thirst.

He stomached cramped into an agonizing ball — like an interior fist that squeezed itself red.

He looked across the darkening ground at the black shafts of grass and wished he could cram his mouth full of hay.

Nearby, Sam let out a long sigh and whined quietly to himself.

"You're hungry too, ain'tcha?" said Hob.

Sam cried softly as if in answer.

A wave of anger crashed over Hob then, momentarily washing away the despair.

"Darn you, King Ketchum," he said. "Darn you and your stupid traps to hell."

When fear came again, it came with a gnawing, relentless delirium.

The day had washed away the hunter. Now Hob was just like the bear. Just like the coyote. Hob was the prey, and he was as lost to himself as to the world.

He was going to die here.

He was sure of it.

Would Ma ever know what became of him?

Would King Ketchum find him? Long after the rains and the field dried to a crusty clay mud, would Hobnail Higgins' bones be half interred therein with the remains of a bear?

While Hob slipped in and out of consciousness, the day turned to night and the rain didn't stop.

He woke up, and he couldn't breathe.

The thundering roar in his ears came from behind and below and all around, and he tried to get his bearings, but couldn't.

Hob gagged on the sour stink of creek

water in his nose and choked as it clogged his throat. His stomach spasmed and he retched up a stream of bile and his arm screamed as his body was pulled parallel with the rushing current.

He struggled through a cave of darkness and was blinded by bolts of bright lightning.

During the night, the creek had overflowed, the swale was flooded nearly two feet deep, and the rush of water across the open field was trying to wrench Hob free of his trap. He flailed in the water, the oncoming waves breaking against his shoulder and rib cage, a battered knee jammed tight against the mud below the surface, his other leg trailing out and away.

Hob tilted his head back and around, water smashing into this forehead, eyes, nose.

He couldn't see Sam anywhere.

The creek washed over him, gray and cold. The agony of his ensnared wrist pounded him back to the fuzzy border between waking and nightmare and he fought to stay aware.

Then Sam was there, right beside him, rolling, barking, panic in his eyes, his massive forelegs thrashing up out of the water.

Hobs was too close. The current had washed him to Sam's side of his own circle.

He tried to push against the floor of the newly created river channel, but his feet washed out from under. He kicked against the mud and the tug of his arm in the trap.

Sam's iron-tough nails raked down through the water and caught Hob on the knee, slicing open the skin like a pocket knife through the red of an apple.

Compared to the pain in his arm, it was nothing.

Filled with terror, he pushed back against the current as hard as he could.

How long he struggled, he had no idea.

In and out of darkness, tossed and turned and twisted by the water.

Half-way in water, he turned his face sideways and in a blast of lightning saw the rifle coming toward him. Rocking up and down, pounding down on him along the surface of the water.

But of course it wasn't the rifle. That had been washed away hours ago.

The long shape barreling toward him, growing longer and larger by the seconds, was a twisted, broke tree branch. And then Hob saw there were other branches lurching through the water as well.

If one of them should smash into his skull . . .

But how would he see them in the dark?

He flipped over into the onrush of water and tried to gauge where the branch was. If only the clouds would light up again. And when they did, if they did — maybe he could —

The branch careened into his back, sending him across the streams toward Sam — wherever he was — whirling — gasping — swallowing too much water.

He was hit again, but this time the branch only scraped his arm.

The next floater was bigger — man-sized. It slammed into his sore arm, but Hob managed to put his weight onto the bow and tip it down.

It spun out of control and bobbed up, knocking him in the chin before it hurried along its way, following the mad torrent.

The water was nearly three feet deep. With his arm stuck in the trap, there was nothing he could do but drown.

Hob rolled over, stopped fighting, and the water pulled him out as far as the chain would allow.

He rode the top of the current that way, floating on his back, avoiding the blunt impact of death by some divine providence.

As the early gray of dawn crawled across the sky, Hob realized he'd survived the night.

To his left, a fat black ball lolled this way and that — half submerged in the water.

Sam!

The rain was coming down more evenly now, in little more than a mist, and Hob watched the bear bob this way and that in the flood water. Not dead, surely? But not alive?

How strangely unreasonable that he, a wastrel of a boy (as Dowd and Stick and the Kempker boys called him) should survive such an ordeal, but a big, strong, denizen of nature be taken away.

It couldn't be true.

The water rushed on as it had all through the night and Hob tried to rouse the bear from his slumber. "S-sam?"

His voice was little more than a mouse's squeak.

"Sam?"

He bent one knee and was able to dip down and touch the slimy ground with a toe.

In spite of the current's tug, or maybe because of its numbing cold, his arm didn't hurt anymore, and Hob was able to navigate toward the bear.

When he got within the radius of Sam's sweeping claws, he hesitated. But there was no motion from the bear.

Hob was near the stake that held Sam's trap in the ground, could thrust his head under water and make out the wavering black shape. It swayed with the river water, loose, but still making a claim in the ground.

"If I could get behind it," thought Hob, "add my weight to the flow of the current . . ."

But of course, the idea wasn't so logically articulated.

Battered, starved, exhausted . . . Hob didn't truly think at all.

Sam was the coyote. The trickster.

This was all some kind of test, wasn't it? Hob narrowed his eyes and grinned.

Of course it was. A trick. A prank. A coyote test.

He pushed himself under and, reaching Sam's anchor, wrapped his good arm around it.

And pushed in the direction of the current.

If one of them should survive, it would be Sam.

Wouldn't that show coyote a thing or two? Hobnail Higgins wasn't so easily fooled.

Hobnail Higgins persevered.

There was great wrenching of the earth then, and another torrent of water hit, and spinning back toward his own circle of terror, Hob fell back into the dark.

The sun stabbed Hob's eyes with light.

Angry, he rolled over and pushed his face into the sloppy wet clay and growled.

"G'way . . ." he said. But the light wouldn't go away.

And something nudged him.

When he tried to move again, the hot pain in his arm forced his eyes open.

Sam's hot breath blew across his forehead from two inches away.

His long pink tongue shot out, dragged through Hob's hairline, reeled itself back in.

The bear's breath smelled like a latrine.

"H-hey . . . S-am."

Hob swallowed hard, realized he was still caught fast . . . but Sam was free.

The clouds had gone and the sky above was a shocking blue.

A gunshot in the distance pushed Sam to his hindlegs. The bear turned away to look up toward the rocky bluff. His nose twitched and the snuffing was as loud as the birdsong coming from the region of the creek.

Hob saw the water was slipping back into its border.

Sam lumbered a few steps back, dragging the chain and iron stake from the clamp on his paw. He looked over his shoulder at Sam, then back toward the bluff as another gunshot rippled through the air.

"Get away there," said a cranky loud voice. "Get on with you." The gunshot again.

Sam gave Hob one last look, a parting glance after all they'd been through together.

Then the bear trundled across the open expanse of the field.

Hob watched him recede back up the trail he'd traveled down the morning before.

Even as King Ketchum hurried toward him, cursing under his breath, asking him if he was okay, Hob kept his eye on Sam's dark shape.

And at the very last, when there was nothing left but a speck and Ketchum knelt down beside him, Hob saw the bear turn into a coyote. He saw the trap slip away from the suddenly narrow hind leg and watched the trickster lope into the tall grass and disappear.

The Second Story Man

Boo Deaver studied the tree, its limp cluster of branches stretched out in the wagon before him, its unfamiliar leaves pale and giving way to autumn. Boo wasn't much of a gardener. As the October wind tugged at his hat, he scratched his beard, then turned toward McGee's store and asked the old man a question. "What kinda tree did you say this was again?"

"Lindenwood," said Moses "Pap" McGee from his wood rocker on the porch. "They grow wild all along the Missouri, and I like the looks of 'em."

"Don't like 'em enough to do your own digging," said Ebby McFarland, leaning on his shovel. "Pulling 'em up, or puttin' 'em back in the ground." He nodded toward the cavity he'd cut in Pap's driveway, "You figure that's deep enough for the thing to take root?"

"Little bit deeper," said Pap before taking

a pull from his flask. "You girls think we're transplanting flowers here?"

"Least you could do is spell me a while." Ebby said, attacking the Nebraska sod with vigor. "Don't know what anybody'd want a darn linden tree for anyway. Soft wood like that ain't good for nothing."

"I ever tell you boys how lindenwood saved my life?" said Pap.

"I'm all ears," said Boo.

Ebby rolled his eyes. "I've heard enough tall tales today," he said. "That story you told us earlier about the cottonwoods was a whopper."

"Well this here is the second story," said Boo.

"A second story about a second story," said Pap. He sat back in his chair with a cackle. "Why that's what you could call me. The second story man."

Boo gave Ebby a wink, and they let Pap spin the yarn.

When I signed on with the McCormick boys to rob the lawyer Smith Whitman's office, I didn't think suffering a rupture was part of the job description. I said so, loud and clear, when the elder brother, Clay McCormick, urged me on.

"Put your back into it, McGee," he said.

"This safe ain't gonna move itself."

What a position I was in: legs akimbo, arms wrapped around the flat back and side of the heavy box safe like a big fat lover. It was late in the evening, and the only light in the office came through the front picture windows from outside where, across the street, the saloon was lit up bright as the noon-day sun. We were pushing the safe away from the light, toward a back window that opened into an alley. Beneath the window, I heard Clay's horse shuffle around where it waited with the wagon I had backed into place earlier.

"I didn't sign up for no hernia," I said. "This damn-blasted thing weighs a ton. Why don't we just bust into the safe, take the loot and scram? Who ever heard of some idiot stealin' the entire damn safe."

Clay pushed the front corner of the lawyer's safe sideways, scraping its squat steel feet on the hard wood floor, nudging it to the left and ahead less than an inch.

"I don't reckon you're helping much," I said. "Where's that danged brother of yours?"

Clay relaxed his grip, stood to his full height of four feet, ten inches, and crossed his arms. "First off, Mick is doing his part of this job, so let's you and me do ours. And in the second place, why we want to take the whole dang safe ain't none of your bidness."

The McCormicks were always talking about bidness.

"You did get the wagon bed reinforced yesterday?" said Clay.

"Brand new oak planks. Just like you asked for," I assured him. "Straight from the sawmill."

"You didn't steal them did you?"

I put on my best hurt look. "The lumber man let me have them on credit. On my mother's Bible," I added. The McCormicks were two of the dirtiest, rottenest scoundrels around, but they were proud of their church going image.

"How much loot you figure is inside anyway?" I said.

"Doesn't matter," said Clay. "Matters is we get it down to the wagon."

Up until this point, I wasn't sure if the McCormicks had come up with this plan on their own, or if they were working for someone. Truth is, I didn't think they were smart enough to come up with any kind of plan on their own. But now, the way I had it figured from the tone of Clay's voice when he answered me, they didn't even know what was in the safe.

I grunted and pushed with all my might. Felt the blood throbbing at my temples.

"Pushing a safe out a second story window," I gasped. "Most foolhardy, dumb—"

"As long as you got that wagon bed reinforced, everything will be fine," said Clay.

Not for the first time, I lamented my dubious reputation as Holt County's strongest man, a reputation I got during a wrestling bout when, under the hot July sun, the other man passed out from heat exhaustion, and I got the credit.

Truth is, I'm a far piece down on the strong man list. And this old iron safe was getting the better of me.

Again Clay put his hands on the safe, grunted a bit, then stood back, this time pulling a big red hanky from his britches. He wiped his forehead and said, "A few more feet and we'll tip it over the edge of the window, drop it into the wagon," said Clay.

"Can't you talk and push at the same time?" I said, panting.

That's when I heard Mick McCormick's voice come from outside.

"Push!" said Clay. Scritch went the safe across the floor.

"Push!" Scritch. The safe inched toward

the window.

Clay's older brother was just below the open window, probably standing near the wagon.

But who was he talking to?

Then I heard Smith Whitman's voice, and a chill passed through me. I couldn't help but stand. "That's the lawyer down there!" I said. "He'll see us."

I lowered my voice to a whisper. "Or hear us," I said.

Clay pooh-poohed me with a wave. "Mick's got it all under control," he said.

"But I can hear them talking," I said.

I could hear both men plainly. They were chatting happily about Whitman's new timber claim up on Oak Creek by one of the new settlements.

"Don't you think Mick ought to get Whitman out of the alley and around the corner?" I said. "We can't steal a man's safe while he stands watching us. That don't work so well."

"Just shut-up and keep pushing," said Clay.

Scritch, scratch, scritch. Another inch.

"Are you boys up to something you're not telling me?" I said.

Scritch, scritch.

Soon they would be able to see us from

the street.

I heard Mick talking about oak trees, the need for a tough blade, the lumber that bent two out of every three nails you tried to drive. Whitman laughed and started talking about lindenwood.

A cool evening breeze trailed through the window.

"Feels nice," I said. Below us, I heard Mick laugh.

"Get on with it you sumbuck," Clay whispered through clenched teeth. I don't know if he meant me or his brother.

Clay leaned against the weight of the safe, really working at it for the first time.

We were only a foot from the open window's edge.

"Hard part's done," said Clay. "Now let's tip 'er up and over."

"Not now we can't," I said. "Not with them down there."

"Mick's got everyone distracted," said Clay.

"No sir," I said. "This is foolhardy."

That's when Clay pulled the little revolver. He held it up like a contest prize for me to see, then shoved it back in his pocket. It wasn't a contest I wanted to win.

"Keep quiet and get ready," he said.

I shut my trap right up and threw away the key.

Together we crouched down, got our fingers under the back edge of the safe and slowly straightened upwards. As a fulcrum point, the window sill could've been worse. It squeaked a little but held, and in less than a minute we had that heavy box balanced, ready to topple out into the reinforced box of the brothers' wagon.

"Hold up, hold up," said Clay.

I shook my head. Within minutes, maybe seconds, Whitman might glance up and, even in the dim moonlight, see the safe perched there with us steadying it from behind.

Down below, the conversation continued.

"As a matter of fact, I just put a new floor in the wagon, said Mick. "Step right up here, Mr. Whitman," he said. Keeping the safe balanced in the window, I couldn't see anything, but it sounded like the men were climbing onto the wagon.

"Right here, Mr. Whitman," said Mick. "Stand right here."

Then he said it again, even louder. "Stand! Right! Here!"

"That's our cue! He ought to be right under us. Let her go," said Clay, pushing the safe forward.

At the last minute, I tried to hold on, but gravity took control of the safe and the weight began to slide.

"Now there's a story I can't even pretend to believe," said Ebby while packing dirt in around the linden tree's root ball.

"What's that supposed to mean?" said Pap, looking offended.

"He don't believe you'd kill anybody," offered Boo. "Everybody knows you're such a soft-hearted cuss."

"That ain't it," said Ebby. "We all know Smith Whitman is still alive and practicing law. But killing him ain't the part I don't believe."

"You probably think I'm too good natured to sign on with them McCormick boys in the first place?" said Pap. "Or maybe you don't believe I was strong enough to hold up my end of the safe?"

"That ain't it either."

"Then what?" said Pap.

"That part about you shutting up and throwing away the key," said Ebby. "That's the part I won't ever believe." Then he burst out laughing.

Boo's smile was as wide and curved as Pap's frown, just in the other direction. "How about we finish packing in this tree, and you tell us how things came out," suggested Boo.

"Yeah, how about you tell us how lindenwood figures into saving your life," said Ebby.

"I was just getting around to that," said Pap.

As the safe toppled into the night, there was nothing I could do to stop it.

I must've had some kind of look on my face, something Clay McCormick could see in the dim light because he laughed at me and said, "This is what they call killing two birds with one stone."

Sure, the plan had been to steal the safe and whatever might happen to be inside, but the goal was to kill Smith Whitman at the same time. And in the off chance the boys were captured, they could claim it was an accident. Maybe even say Whitman had hired them to move the safe.

From below came the crash.

And then silence.

I leaned out the window to take a look. The floor of the wagon was broken clean through, and the safe rested there cockeyed: part on the ground, part still stuck in the splintered wagon floor. Clay's horse complained and danced around, but the wagon was held fast by the heavy safe in its sunken bird's nest of splintered soft wood.

"What happened?" said Clay. "What happened?" He joined me at the window, then stepped back to swat me with his hat.

"Dummy! You told me you put oak in that wagon. That ain't oak!"

That's when I pulled my own small revolver from my britches and held it on him.

"You okay down there, Mr. Whitman?" I called out.

Clay walked back to the window, and I followed him. We both saw Whitman safely off to the side, his gun squarely on Mick McCormick.

"Bring him on down, McGee," said Whitman.

Clay took a step away from the window and spread his arms out.

"I don't understand," he said.

"Whitman got wind of your plan a few days back. Seems that after you visited the lawyer in order to scope the place out, you talked a little too much over at the saloon. Pretty much gave the whole thing away before it had even begun."

"So you were in on it the whole time? You did all that pushing just to help put me and my brother behind bars?"

"I reckon I did," I said. "Smith hired me

for the same reason you boys did. Tales of my own strength have been greatly exaggerated."

Clay rubbed the back of his head while I urged him on downstairs at gunpoint.

"I still don't get what happened with the wagon," he said.

"I don't either," said Ebby.

Boo looked expectantly at Pap rocking back and forth on the porch. "What do you think of the tree?"

Pap stood and leaned against the porch rail, admiring the newly planted tree.

"Looks fine, boys. How about you join me inside for a warm shot of something to take the chill off?"

"I still want to know how the lindenwood saved your life," said Ebby.

"The thing is," said Pap, "The man at the sawmill let me have the linden wood on the cheap because nobody really wants the stuff. I honestly didn't figure it would matter that much. I knew it was a soft wood, but I didn't think the safe would go right through."

"But you're happy it did?" said Boo as he and Ebby stepped onto the porch.

"Darn happy," said Pap, opening the door to the store. "Remember how I didn't know what was inside the safe? How I suspected the brothers didn't know either? Well, it turns out it was full of confiscated owlhoot dynamite. Sweaty, touchy old dynamite."

"Had the impact of that safe been just a tad more jarring . . . ," began Ebby.

"We might've been high as the second story real permanent-like. Sitting on a cloud with angel wings," said Pap.

"Angel wings on Pap McGee," said Ebby. "Now there's another thing I can't believe."

Chuckling to himself, Boo slapped his friends on the back and followed them into the store.

Police Escort

At Dodge House, Billy slugged the man behind the counter, helped himself to Room Three's box of jewelry, then strolled out through the kitchen and into the back alley. With cool forethought he'd noticed a horse and wagon parked there on his way in, so now he pushed the box under a canvas cover, climbed into the seat, and drove through shade toward the edge of Taylorville. On a lazy Sunday afternoon halfway into August, with everybody visiting relatives or down at the ice cream social, nobody paid him two cents' worth of attention, least of all the resident of Room Three. Billy heard she was the wife of some local politician. Well, she probably already had more than her share of fancy pins and rings and necklaces.

That night Billy made a cold camp under the stars beside a secluded creek. The next morning, he pulled out early without breakfast and started through the sandhills, headed for Grand Lake, where he'd pick up the Burlington and Missouri River train.

On the downhill side of an especially steep grade, a girl stumbled out of a shadowy blowout onto the trail ahead of him. She almost fell in the heavy dust, and Billy would've run her down if he hadn't pulled back hard on the reins. The horse reluctantly obeyed, bringing the wagon creaking to a halt.

"Damnation lady," said Billy, but clipped his words short when he saw what she carried.

A kid in a basket, not more than a year old, wrapped in a heavy quilt. All Billy could see was part of the baby's face.

The girl, long haired and slim, put the basket on the ground and rubbed her forehead, smearing it with sweaty sand.

"Help me, mister," she said. Her lips weren't chapped, but it sounded like she hadn't had a drink in quite a spell.

"Sorta hot for that quilt ain't it?" said Billy, nodding at the baby.

"We gotta get to a doctor," said the girl.

Billy rubbed the side of his head and considered the situation.

"Where'd you come from?" he said.

"Back yonder," she said. "Got a shack. A

claim. My man's been gone two weeks. He was supposed to be bringin' food. Medicine. Now Lila's sick."

"Lila? That's the kid?"

The girl nodded. "We can't wait no more, mister."

The girl's red hair was plastered to her face, and her eyes were going every which way, but those long legs, that thin skirt and loose cotton blouse brought words to Billy's mouth before he knew it.

"Let me give you a lift," he said, climbing down to help.

"Oh God bless you, mister."

"Already has," said Billy with a smile. "What's your name then?"

"Name is Beth," said the girl. "Just Beth."

"Well Missuz Beth, let's get you and Lila some help."

With his passengers situated, Billy snapped the reins and the horse took them around the next hill.

Nodding at the basket in Beth's lap, Billy said, "What's wrong with her?"

"I don't know. She's sick."

From what Billy could see showing beneath the quilt the kid looked kind of pasty. And dreadful quiet. When a sick baby don't bawl, it meant real trouble. With three bratty sisters back home, Billy knew that much.

"Nearest doc is over at Mary's Home," he said. "Take us 'til noon to get there, and it's in the wrong direction."

"Wrong direction?"

"If the doc ain't in, we're stuck in the middle of nowhere. It'll take us all day, but I think we ought to try for Grand Lake. Spunky little railroad town."

"Whatever you think."

"My name's Billy, by the way."

"God bless you, Billy."

The rode a while under the morning sun.

Then Billy said, "How old is your Lila?"

Beth turned away, acted like she hadn't heard him.

"I suspect it's a handful raising a child way out here."

Once more, Beth didn't answer.

When enough time had passed, Billy tried again.

"Lila born out here?"

"Look here," said Beth, "she's not mine, alright? I'm just watching her for a friend."

Oh, so!

Billy inflated his cheeks, blew out with a whistle.

"We'd best stop right here," he said, but Beth put her hand on his leg.

"Please don't," she said. "Lila needs that doctor."

"You runnin' away, ma'am?"

"Let's say it's not your business."

"Let's say I don't want your husband coming up behind us."

"He won't," Beth said. Her green eyes met his and held them. "My husband and me ain't exactly together anymore. Doubt we'll ever be together like we was. Never again."

"Never again?"

"You understand?" she said, and her smile triggered a chill that swept down his sun-baked form.

Hot damn. What had he got himself into?

"Just get us to Grand Lake," said Beth, now more like an order than a request.

Billy thought about the box of jewels riding along behind them. Despite his passengers, the good long ride away from Taylorville suited him fine. He'd gotten out of town clean, but by now the rickety old sheriff would probably be after him. The only good part of that was that the sheriff would most likely be alone. There just weren't that many folks available in Taylorville for a posse.

Well, they wouldn't be looking for a man with a woman and a baby.

Billy shouted the horse into a gallop, and the wagon jerked forward.

They bounced over pincushion plants and skeleton weeds for more than a mile. "Lots of hard going through these parts," said Billy, working the reins with both hands.

Then the road smoothed out some and Beth tilted her head back against the late afternoon sun. "Sure could use a smoke," she said.

"Me too," said Billy, but he was out of the makings.

"Between you and me," she said, "whatever's wrong with Lila, I can't pay for no medicine. I got nothing to my name. Not now."

Billy knew when to stop asking questions. Soon as they got to the outskirts of Grand Lake, he was dropping Beth and Lila like the poison they were. Thinking about it, he decided he was just gonna keep riding. Head for the Wyoming border.

Helping himself to some rich biddy's box of frew-fraws was one thing. Helping out a mankiller was another.

But he had a soft spot for kids. What would happen to Lila?

"Don't worry about money," he said.

"Oh, you got a rich uncle?" said Beth.

"I can maybe help a little. When we get to town."

That's when the lone rider came out of

the sun and crossed their path. Something in the combination of Stetson and spurs, riding chaps, and pearl handled revolvers said "law man" even before Billy saw the glint of a tin star on the man's chest.

"Oh no, that's — ," said Beth. "Oh no," she whispered again, bowing low to tend the baby, adjusting the quilt as the horse approached.

"Oh, Billy," she said. "Don't stop."

The rider passed them, then circled around with a wave and followed behind as Billy rolled on.

"Better if I do," he said.

"Can't you outrun him?"

"Three of us on a wagon?" said Billy.

"It's just that I don't want to delay. Poor Lila . . . ," Beth's words trailed off.

"Poor Lila is our way out of this," said Billy. "You just sit tight."

Billy pulled over and set the brake on the wagon as the horse came up along the side. The rider was young. Younger than Billy, with a bushy mustache and wearing a heavy coat of Bay Rum cologne. Billy didn't know the man, but recognized the badge. United States Marshal.

"You folks raise more dust than a herd o' gophers. Liable to bust up your wagon driving that way," said the marshal. "This old snaky road gets mighty treacherous up ahead."

Billy let the words come as fast as he could think them up.

"Got a sick baby, sir. We don't make Grand Lake by dark, I don't know what we'll do."

The marshal peered across the wagon at Beth and Lila.

"What seems to be the trouble?" he said.

"Fever. Heavy breathing. You gotta help us mister," said Beth.

"Like you was saying," said Billy, "it gets mighty treacherous up ahead."

The marshal seemed to be thinking over the situation. Billy smiled to himself. No doubt the decision would be easier if the lawman saw what was under the canvas in back.

Maybe word from Taylorville hadn't gotten out this far. Or maybe it had.

"You two ain't happened across a lone stranger on the road? Young fellow traveling alone out of Taylorville?"

"Ain't seen nobody," said Billy. "Me and my wife left our claim just this morning."

"Where'd you say you was headed?"

"Grand Lake."

"I know a short-cut. You follow me," said the marshal.

"That would be Jim-dandy," said Billy. "Jim-dandy indeed."

Billy let the horse and wagon fall in behind the law man.

"Now we got the law on our side," said Billy. "There's irony here, Beth, that's what there is."

"What's irony?" said Beth.

"Dumb luck," said Billy with a forced laugh. "Little Lila there is our good luck charm."

"I go where the law leads me," said Billy, and this time his laugh was more genuine. "Ain't that a hoot, Beth?"

"Mind your horse, Billy," said Beth.

"See that's the thing," said Billy. "It ain't even my horse. I ain't just a jewel thief," he said.

"Jewel thief?" said Beth, and Billy sobered up fast.

"Look here, Beth," he began.

"No, I want to hear more," said Beth. "A girl likes to hear a man talk about jewels."

Ahead, the marshal rode fast in a cloud of yellow sand that suddenly looked like roaring tongues of fire.

"Lot of curves, this part of the road," said Beth. "Be careful, huh?"

"I been driving a wagon since I was a sprout," said Billy.

"About them jewels? About what you said?"

On the tight curves, the wagon rolled from side to side.

"You rob a bank or something?" said Beth.

"I'm not a bank robber," said Billy.

"But you got something going on," said Beth.

"How about we just get Lila to the doc in one piece?"

"I just thought I could help you if you were in trouble. Maybe we could help each other."

Billy squinted into the dust, could make out the marshal's progress as he led them into increasingly unfamiliar territory. They were headed the right direction to make Grand Lake, but Billy didn't know the road.

"Well now, I ain't necessarily in trouble," said Billy, cautious with his words. "Did I give you that idea?"

"You did," said Beth, nodding.

"A God-fearing husband with his wife and sick daughter? Bein' escorted by a representative of the law? I got nothing in the world to be afeared of."

"You said you were a jewel thief."

Billy grinned but kept quiet.

"Oh Billy, I told you my secret. About Lila I mean."

The marshal went around another hill, and Billy followed. He glanced down at Lila, sleeping in the basket under the heavy quilt, then let his eyes move up and linger over Beth's torso, the loose buttons of her blouse, the bare, freckled neck underneath.

"Alright," he said. "It was like this. I left Omaha in the spring. Been drifting for better than a month between jobs. I laid over in Taylorville and lost my horse in a poker game."

"You don't look like no gambler I ever saw."

"I took a gamble on you, didn't I, Beth?"

Beth's eyes twinkled in the sun. "Go on," she said.

"So during the game, one of them owlhoots said the wife of a local fellar was in town, staying at the hotel. Said she left a box of jewels with the front desk."

"Mighty careless," said Beth. "I would've kept it with me."

"Well, she probably figured it was more safe with the desk."

"Probably."

"But see, it wasn't. Yesterday afternoon, nobody around, I just helped myself."

"You got the jewels here?" said Beth, turning around to look in the wagon bed.

Billy shook his head. "Don't you worry

about," he said. "I think —"

Beth followed his gaze and held her breath. Perpendicular to their course, another horseman was riding in on them hard. The angle of his descent would land him directly in their path, but behind the marshal.

Cutting them off.

"Who's this now?" said Beth.

"Sheriff," said Billy. "Old bachelor from Taylorville I'll bet."

"Did the marshal see him?"

"Don't think so."

"Veer off, Billy."

"Shut up," said Billy,

Now he could see that it was the old Taylorville sheriff, his stringbean body swaying in a broke down saddle.

"Have to stop," he said, more to himself than to Beth. "Keep your mouth shut and ears open."

"Ho there," said Sheriff Dawson. "Ho, now."

Billy let the wagon roll to a stop. Sweat ran down his face, but his mouth was dry as the landscape around them.

"Where you going in such a hurry, son?" said Dawson.

"Doctor," said Billy. "We've got a sick child."

"That so?"

"That's right," said Billy. "Even got us an escort," he added.

And just like that, the marshal appeared. He rode up to the sheriff.

"Afternoon," he nodded. "I'm Marshal —"

"I know who you are," said Dawson. "What goes on here? I'm looking for a jewel thief."

"I can appreciate that," said the Marshal, "but I'm taking these folks across Banner's Way to Grand Lake. Got to get the child to a doctor."

Dawson nodded.

Banner's Way.

Billy thought it sounded familiar.

"I'm headed that way myself. Mind if I follow you?"

Billy swallowed hard, saw Beth was about to say something, and shook his head.

"Suit yourself," said the marshal. Then he called to the wagon. "That baby okay?"

"We need to move along right now," said Beth. "We can't wait any more."

"That's sort of what I was thinking. Follow me."

Billy snapped the reins and drove the wagon in the marshal's wake.

Dawson fell in behind the wagon like a

swinging gate.

Ahead, the marshal was cantering slow.

They passed a sign that read Banner's Way.

Around the hill, and they rode toward a small shack surrounded with stacks of wood and a few outside barrels.

Banner's Way was a railroad station, small, but still a railroad station. Tracks stretched left and right into the distance.

The marshal arrived at the shack and dismounted.

"What in thunder?" said Billy.

"Looks like we took a short cut after all," said Beth.

"Short cut to the rails, not a doctor," said Billy.

"I don't think we need a doctor to ship you back to Omaha," said Beth.

"We? Omaha?"

Billy stared at the gun Beth pulled from under the quilt in Lila's basket.

"Train ought to be along any time now," she said.

Billy turned his head from right to left. The sheriff stood at the side of the wagon.

"C'mon down, son. The marshal will get you home."

"Who are you people?"

"Name is Virgil Harm," said the marshal. "The lady there is my wife."

"What about . . . ," Billy wrinkled his forehead. "What about Lila?"

Beth smiled while she pulled the quilt away to reveal a life-like wax doll's head with no body attached to it.

Billy shook his head. He knew that baby'd been unnatural quiet.

He stepped to the ground with the sound of the train whistle in the distance.

"Looks like your jewels are all here, honey" said Harm, stepping away from the wagon.

"Good for you, Billy," said Beth.

"Your jewels? Then you're the —"

"Wife of the local politician. Only he's not a politician. He's a U. S. Marshal. And you're Billy Dunn, wanted for federal revenue fraud."

Harm shook Dawson's hand. "Sure do appreciate the support."

"Hard to raise a posse out here. Wouldn't be good for one man to go it alone."

"I'll be okay on the train," said Harm.

Billy felt the afternoon sun burning into him.

Felt like he was coming down with something.

"I may need a doc myself," he murmured as the train came into view.

"Omaha is a good long ride," said Beth.

"But at least you'll get a police escort."

"It's the least we can do," said Marshal Harm.

Branham's Due

Deputy Whit Branham found the border collie half-starved and parched to the bone, trapped in loose barbed wire near the old trapper's soddie at Iron Creek. How long the poor devil had been hung up was anyone's guess, but the wounds looked superficial and there wasn't much blood. "Just enough to hurt like the dickens, I'll bet," he told the dog. The collie turned away, but not before giving Whit a shamed look in reply. "No need to be embarrassed, boy," said Whit. "It can happen to the best of us."

Barbed wire fences were a bit of a novelty in Holt County, Nebraska, but they'd also been around long enough for folks to learn how to stretch a wire. The half-assed job Whit had been riding beside sure enough slowed down the dog, but it would never stand up to a hungry half-ton of beef looking for new grass on the ragged land north of O'Neill City.

Last he knew, this naked range was unclaimed, but times were changing fast. The railroad carried a steady stream of homesteaders, folks hailing from hell to thunder, all of 'em strangers, all of 'em looking for profit or gain. It was hard on a man who didn't like change, someone who'd spent a lot of time figuring out the way things were. Whit Branham was such a man.

While Whit freed the dog, his big Percheron gelding, Lubber, made impatient noises on the trail. With a leather glove, Whit gripped the top braid of wire between its barbs and, with a solid effort, pulled it free of its anchor. The middle and lowest strand gave way under the simple weight of his boot.

At that, the dog rolled forward and came alive, leaping up with a healthy shake. "Bet that feels good," said Whit, one hand at his hip, the other tipping back his crumpled straw hat. The dog tasted the late winter air, and Whit thought it was as close to a grateful smile as he was going to come all day.

The dog spun in a quick circle, barked once, and ran in the direction of the sod house before vanishing in a broken stand of bluestem at the creek's edge.

Whit walked back to his horse, the tin star on his heavy flannel coat glinting in the morning sun. He knew Johann Kramer was in that soddie, and he aimed to get him.

Johann Kramer of Dakota Territory, armed with the hot Colt he used to set the Black Hills against him and a hard empty place where his conscience should've been. He was a horse-thief and known killer.

Taking one last look after the dog, Whit pulled a short Stevens 10-gauge from the saddle boot and slung it over his shoulder. He was burning daylight.

Whit recalled the last time he'd been past the abandoned shelter where Kramer was holed up. If he approached from the creek bed behind the soddie and a little to the west, he'd be on the side opposite the old wood stove. Cold as it was, Kramer would probably be close to the heat, maybe still in bed sleeping off the night before. Whit didn't think the outlaw had much to do with Sunday mornings.

Leading Lubber through a wide, snow-dappled shallow into the low, trickling stream, Whit caught the scent of smoke, thought he made out a thread of gray in the sky.

He and Barney Kearns, Holt County sheriff, had learned Kramer was on the prod in O'Neill an hour too late. By the time they got to Kramer's watering hole, the barkeep was all but shuttering the windows. With a full moon just beginning to wane, Kearns suggested tracking Kramer over the frozen prairie, but as they talked, a cardsharp with a grudge gave up the secret of the old Iron Creek sod hovel where the wanted man had been hiding for more than a week. The lawmen agreed to ride out at first light.

Part of Whit's job was to make sure the sheriff of Holt County didn't get killed. Especially not by some gunny in short pants who wasn't half the man Kearns was. Whit woke early and, one last time before heading out, studied the reward card for Kramer along with a report from the Dakota Territory. No use bringing in the wrong man.

At thirty-two, Whit had yet to lose the confidence of youth. He knew the land and thought he knew Kramer well enough. Splashing along, Whit eventually saw some early sprigs of bright green poking through the thin snow crust at the water's edge. With a length of canvas, he put together a quick hobble for Lubber. "Don't go anywhere," he said, stroking the big boy's short mane.

He climbed over melting slick ice and mud, remembering the names of Kramer's victims from the report: Jack Wilson, Kevin Mark, Neil Marvin, Matthew Daniels. Not one of them more than twenty years old, none of them old enough to stake a real claim on life. Not one of them deserving what he got.

Once Whit made the creek bank, he pounded forward, swinging the shotgun to the front of his body. At less than fifty yards out, a pale, thin, watery-eyed Johann Kramer came around the edge of soddie whistling, "Katy Bell." Shirtless and barefoot, Kramer stumbled backward when he saw Whit.

"Whoa, hoss," he said.

"Johann Kramer?" said Whit.

"Who're you?" said Kramer.

"Deputy sheriff," said Whit. "Come to take you in, son."

"Don't that beat all?" said Kramer. "Calling me son and can't be more than a few years older."

Whit's eyes were tough-jacketed slugs pressing his quarry. "Get yourself dressed," he advised, and together they walked around the corner of the house.

Whit didn't see the dog until Kramer made an awkward lunge sideways with a cry of "Get him!"

Whit rocked back and steadied himself for an attack that never came. Languid and amiable, the border collie he'd rescued from the fence raised its hindquarters and stretched before shaking off a short nap.

"Get 'im, dog!" said Kramer again.

The dog ambled over. Cradling the shotgun in his left elbow, Whit ruffled the collie's ears. "Looks like guard duty doesn't quite suit him."

At the creaking, open door of the soddie, Kramer looked crestfallen. "You shoulda seen him take after this old boy in the sandhills last month," he said.

"You two travelin' together?" said Whit.

Kramer said they were and scratched his head in annoyance. "I just can't figure it," he said as he watched the dog lap Whit's hand.

"Let's get a move on," said Whit, motioning toward the open door. Whit lowered his head and kept his eyes wide as he followed Kramer into the dim interior, the shotgun square with the outlaw's back.

The collie padded into the dirt room and turned around three times before settling down on a straw mattress beside an iron stove. The stove's open door showed a few embers from the grass pile smoldering there. Might've been a good fire given the chance. An impressive pile of kindling and firewood was stacked in the corner.

"Dog got a name?" asked Whit.

"Still ain't decided," said Kramer, quickly

slipping on a pair of boots. "Something rough-sounding."

As he buttoned his shirt, Kramer moved along the soddies's long wall opposite the lawman. Whit kept the conversation going, paralleling the man's moves. "How about Leonard?" he suggested.

"Leonard ain't rough-sounding," said Kramer. "Why Leonard?"

"Knew an old trapper named Leonard," said Whit, stepping around the mattress, circling toward Kramer. "Used to live in this very house."

"That a fact?" said Kramer, stopping next to the end wall of earthen blocks.

Whit shoved between Kramer and the wall even as he lunged forward. Kramer clawed at the soft earth, managed only to nudge away a fraction of an inch before Whit slammed the reversed shotgun into his ribs. Reeling back from the heavy wood stock, Kramer landed on the floor with a thud.

With the back of his hand, Whit knocked away the remainder of the hidey hole's false front. Inside, on a floor of sanded oak, he found Kramer's famed Navy Colt. "This what you wanted?" he said, drawing it out and shoving it into this own belt.

"You knew?" Kramer gasped, struggling to catch his breath.

"I've lived around here a long time," said Whit. "Know a lot of people and a lot of secrets."

"My unlucky day," said Kramer, climbing carefully to his feet while Whit removed a long piece of twine from the pocket of his pants.

"I mean, first the dog, now the house. You seem to be one step ahead of me, mister," said Kramer.

"You got to give the devil his due," said Whit as he bound Kramer's wrists together behind his back.

"Oh, I always do," said Kramer, and his grin was just a little too wide. "But I've also beat him a time or two."

From an oak peg buried in the wall, Whit pulled down a battered hat, tossed it onto the man's head. "Don't want you catching cold."

"Let's just get on with it," said Kramer, shuffling out the door in boots that seemed at least two sizes too big.

Johann Kramer, unlucky horse thief and known killer, pale, thin and watery-eyed, was coming along too peaceably. He'd tried to sic the dog on Whit and, yes, he'd gone for his gun. But the way he moved now, half-hearted, like all the starch was boiled out of him, just didn't seem right. Whit thought Kramer probably had one more ace up his sleeve. Maybe had something to do with those squishy too-big boots.

The collie trailed along behind.

Whit never discounted luck: he'd been lawing too long for that. But a good helping of luck didn't mean squat if you didn't know what to do with it. His eyes took in every detail, and his fingers were loose but ready on the Stevens.

When they got to the creek, Lubber hadn't strayed more than a few feet from where Whit had left him. The deputy helped Kramer mount the saddle, then started them back the way he'd come, aiming for the barbed wire trail leading across the range to O'Neill. He sniffed the air again. The smoke he smelled in the creek bottom might have drifted along from the soddie. Or had it been tobacco smoke? Another whiff and it was gone.

The prisoner played his last card as they made the ridge out of Iron Creek.

A big block of a woman was crouched down, trying to hide in the grass. The collie yipped, bouncing into the dormant brome.

"Drop the —" the woman started to say, but Whit had been ready. He let the scatter-gun explode, sending a hard bloom of fire into the air above. The woman tossed an old cap and ball pistol toward Whit's feet and hauled herself off the ground. She wore a long, wool nightshirt and a baggy pair of men's pants. Her bare, brick feet didn't seem to need much protection.

Whit bit his tongue.

"Dammit, Darla," said Kramer. "What kind of rescue was that?"

The woman mopped her forehead. "Are you wearing my boots?" she said.

"I was in a hurry," said Kramer.

She paused, then wet her lips. "Well I'll be dipped in vinegar," said Darla. "Whit Branham! What you doin' out here?"

This just wasn't Johann Kramer's day.

"How you been, Darla?" he said, smiling into the woman's big pumpkin face, her ruddy skin and missing teeth clear memories from more than a decade before.

"I been good, Whit!" said the giantess. She stuck her tongue out when a happy laugh turned to coughing. "I'm sorry," she said. "Got to lay off the tobaccy."

"By golly, it's good to see you Dar," said Whit.

From Lubber's back, Kramer mumbled. "You two know each other?"

"Know each other?" bawled Darla. "Me and Whit practically grew up together down on the South Platte." She leaned into Whit and laid a meaty arm on his shoulder. "Them were some days."

"They were indeed," Whit agreed. "You remember ol' Lars Johnson?"

Darla nodded.

"Married Beth Streeter," Whit told her.

"I can't believe it!" said Darla. "Not old Lars!"

"There was a time," Whit told Kramer, "Darla was my Sunday school teacher."

"Sunday school teacher?" said Kramer. The outlaw's features practically fell into his lap.

Whit raised his eyebrows, bobbing his head quickly. "That's right."

Darla laughed out loud. "I can't believe you remember," she said.

Kramer groaned.

"Devil his due," said Whit.

"You're lucky it was me out here," said Darla.

Whit started to reply, but the big woman cut him off. "Anybody else would've killed you on the spot."

With that, she dropped the butt of a second pistol across the back of Whit's head, sending him face first into the prickly hardpan.

■ ■ ■ ■

When he woke, their positions were reversed.

Whit found himself riding the horse, his wrists tied tight behind his back, while Johann Kramer walked barefoot beside Darla of the monstrous boots. Needing to think, Whit pushed his eyes shut, pretended to be asleep.

Hard to think when you are chewing yourself up inside. He'd been duped like a newborn calf.

Below him, his captors argued as they led Lubber across a stubble field toward the horizon.

"I say we put a bullet in him," said Kramer.

"I can't shoot somebody I taught Bible," said Darla. "A person oughta have a scruple, and that's mine."

"I've killed better mothers' sons than him," said Kramer.

At the boast, the names of Kramer's victims floated back into Whit's mind, phantoms with a message for Whit if he could decipher it, specters with a vengeance, with a way to beat their killer. Whit struggled to recall every detail of Kramer's report.

"Lord, I wish I had a smoke," said Darla. "Feels like I got ants crawlin' on me."

"We can get supplies up at the river crossing," said Kramer.

"Good place to leave Branham," said Darla.

"I don't know why you're so afraid of killing him," said Kramer.

From the back of his horse, Whit said, "I've got some tobacco here in my shirt pocket, Dar."

Kramer drew reign on Lubber. A few hundred feet ahead, the collie noticed the party's lack of progress and started circling back toward them.

Whit said, "I got rolling paper, too."

"I don't think so, Branham," said Kramer.

"I told you this one was worth keeping around," said Darla. "Bring him down here."

Kramer jerked the Colt from his holster and started waving it around like a crochet hook.

"It's a trick," he said. "He comes down here, I'm not responsible for what happens."

Towering over her boyfriend and shaking with nicotine withdrawal, Darla thrust the Stevens straight into his groin. "If he don't get down here, you won't be responsible for much of anything."

Anger snapping off every move, Kramer jerked Whit from the saddle, levered him up, then knocked him back into the side of his horse.

Tall, wide-shouldered, slender at the hip, with his hands tied behind his back, Whit righted himself and faced Johann Kramer and his wavering Colt. He knew he could lick him.

Darla checked the pockets of his coat and shirt. "You were right, honey bun," she said. "He ain't got nothin' in his pockets."

Whit couldn't hide a sheepish look. "Sorry, Dar," he said.

"Damn you, Whit," she said. "I've a notion to lay a gun upside your head again."

"If you won't shoot me, why not cut me loose?" he said.

"See?" said Kramer. "Just like I said."

With menace in his voice, Whit shuffled into the Colt's muzzle. "Well, all right then, son," emphasizing the last word. "Go ahead and shoot."

Kramer hesitated. "I'll do it," he said, but he was starting to tremble. "By God, I'll do it."

Whit could barely stand still, blood racing through his frame, his Irish eyes a copper green fire.

The report from Dakota, the one with the

list of Kramer's victims, had been clear, precise to the last detail.

Jack Wilson, 17, shot in the back.

Kevin Mark, 19, shot in the back.

Neil Marvin, 18, shot in the back.

Whit unleashed his fury. "You come in to my county, sneak around the same gutless way you did in the Black Hills. You think you know something because you've been here a spell, maybe met a few people. Well, you don't know nothing." The Colt still pressed into his belly, Whit pushed Kramer back.

"But I know you," he said.

Matthew Daniels, 19, shot in the back.

"You can't kill a man face-to-face, can you, Kramer? You can't look in his eye and pull the trigger. If you could, you'd do it now and empty my guts to the ground."

"Shoot him, Darla," said Kramer. "Shoot him!"

Big Darla stepped forward, got between Whit and the gun.

"I'll untie you, Whit," she said.

"Don't bother," said Whit, raising his leg high, striking out at Kramer's scrawny knee, remembering how the barbed wires had snapped under that same boot.

Whit made sure Darla was bound snug as

Kramer, but they walked together easily on the way back to O'Neill while the killer sat in the saddle. With a broken knee and only half conscious, Kramer was in no shape for a stroll.

The sun was high over the bristly scrub, the breeze promising spring.

"You forgive me, Whit?" said Darla.

"I don't know, girl," said Whit. "Forgiveness has never been my strong suit. You might recall I flunked Sunday school."

"I think you did fine."

They walked a while in silence. Finally, Darla said, "You took an awful chance back there."

Whit glanced back at Kramer.

"Give the devil his due, Darla," said Whit.

"Just one thing I can't figure," said Darla.

"What's that?"

How you knew Johann was out of bullets," said Darla.

"Out of bullets," whispered Whit to himself.

"Otherwise he'd a plugged you for sure."

Far ahead the collie barked a happy note across the plains, a note not nearly as grateful as one Whit Branham whistled softly to himself.

Founders' Song

West across the sandhills in that part of Nebraska, there was nothing to look at but the odd rumpled dunes, scrub brush and the sky. Coburn straightened in his saddle. His back answered with a crackling volley of sound. As much as he enjoyed the dry brace of late summer air and the quiet solitude of his surroundings, he was ready for a change. Since early morning, when he'd watched a duck take ragged flight from its concealed wetland home, he'd seen little that passed for life. The rabbit he might've bagged for supper was especially coy. Everything had gone to ground; even the buckskin he rode was acting like he'd rather be somewhere else. Change, he suspected, was coming soon enough.

He smelled the storm, earthy and wet, before he saw it. At the next summit he took in a panoramic view of towering white clouds atop a blue-black strata that pressed to the horizon. Twenty paces away, a washout offered shelter. Coburn headed toward it, confident for once that he had the jump on Mother Nature. When the first howling breath of cold went past, he and the horse were hunkered down well.

"Stay still now, ya bumblehead," he advised, and the buckskin snorted into the oncoming gale.

A fussbudget of a storm, long on wind, lightning and noise, short on precipitation. He'd seen more water birthing calves. As quick as they came, the clouds drew back, and just over the next hill the sun caught something white, a reflection especially bright, deliberately drawing his eye.

In the rough terrain of this so-called Great American Desert, settlements were still sparse as wild strawberries, but that didn't mean people weren't cussed stubborn enough to try and make a home. Eyes narrowed, Coburn could make out a few buildings, some dugouts, and a scattered pile of wood. Looked like there might've been some wind damage.

Rubbing his chin thoughtfully, he talked to his horse. "Shall we see what's going on or press on for a while?" The buckskin whinnied.

"Ah, hell," Coburn said. "I got enough

trouble." The horse danced lightly toward the place, shaking its head as if to disagree. They were traveling north toward Dakota, more or less; it wasn't like he had anywhere else to be. Between jobs, he carried plenty of provisions, had water to spare, money in his pockets and plenty of time to explore the country, letting nature and fool-headed horses take their course.

"Damn do-gooder," he said, turning in the saddle and setting off at a safe trot toward the small settlement. The horse could have his way, but Corburn wasn't going to hurry.

Up and down across the dunes, the closer Coburn got, the more he wondered about the place. The damage he'd seen was near a pair of wood frame houses. Scattered timber and splinters of every size decorated the ground, the remnants of a horse corral. To the west a couple of gray shacks leaned into the wind, and a small soddie tilted under its own weight. Something less than a road, but more than a cow trail meandered through it all. The railroad was a good distance away where the Sioux City and Pacific stopped at Valentine. Whoever lived here was mighty ambitious — overly so, from the looks of things. Much as he enjoyed the country, it was hard to believe anyone would fight to set down roots here. And in fact, the buildings appeared to be deserted. Another false start on the westward way toward the future.

He pushed the horse into a run when he saw a body lying dead in the sand.

But the kid wasn't dead. Overcome by the storm, or maybe by malnutrition from the looks of her scrawny arms and legs, she was alive, breathing, coughing up chunks of bile as Coburn helped her into a sitting position.

The large gray home was a tidy affair, complete with a porch, decorative eves, and a small shack in the yard. Glass windows in both structures were cloudy but whole. The buckskin shied back, so Coburn led it aside, picking his way through the torn wood remains of the corral. He flipped the reigns around a fence post and continued to look around. The sturdy pens, intact but empty, looked like they hadn't ever been used.

"Some storm," he said, not sure the girl was listening. "You're lucky it didn't take your house." Somebody coughed as he said it. Coughed again. Feminine, but not weak.

"Ma's in the shed," said the girl. The shack door swung open for someone lugging out a heavy wet bag.

"Lindy?" she yelled, then coughed again.

"Belinda Sue?"

"Here, mama," said the girl. Coburn helped her stand, then went to help the older woman. You couldn't see it from the front, but part of the shack's roof was gone, fallen in on a store of flour and grain.

"Let me give you a hand," said Coburn. The woman nodded, and together they salvaged the contents of the shack.

Ignoring their work, the sun slid down toward the earth.

At the supper table, Emma Hessler gave thanks before passing him a biscuit smothered in watery beans. "It's not much," she said, "but we're obliged to you, Mr. Coburn."

"I'll do more tomorrow," he said.

The interior of the house was neatly arranged, despite layers of dust and mud-dobbers circling overhead.

"That a real gun on your hip?" said Lindy. "You supposed to be a gunslinger?"

"Yes it is, and no I'm not," he answered.

"Maybe tomorrow you could show me how to shoot."

"Got to clean up that mess of a corral tomorrow."

Lindy pouted over her plate, fell back in her chair. "I hate guns anyway," she said, matter-of-factly.

"I wish you wouldn't worry yourself," said Emma. "We've put you out long enough."

"Oh, mother," Lindy said. The girl was sallow, petulant and not very pretty. Coburn put her at eighteen, thinking she might be younger than she looked. The wind added years but not necessarily wisdom. Dumb as a hammer.

Emma was a different story. It wasn't just a school marm's book smarts that shaped her chiseled, weather-burned features, but a sense of competence, of real world experience that should have appealed to him. But something about her made his neck itch.

Coburn worked through the tasteless grub without saying much.

When they were finished, Emma handed him a tin of weak coffee and led him into a room full of books. Like his two hosts, the shelves presented a contrast; curving wood held scores of volumes organized alphabetically by author, but their spines were sun-bleached and worn. At the window, a dozen flies buzzed, their speckled leavings painting the glass.

Plato, Shakespeare, Charles Dickens. When he cracked open a copy of *The Tempest,* a half-dozen silverfish darted every which way. He laid the book down and smiled at his host.

Emma picked up the clothbound book, its cover twisting loose in her hands. Her eyes sparkled when she spoke.

"Seems to me you've been here a while," he said.

"Long enough to call it our own," Emma said, her chin tilting up with unexpected defiance. "I live here, in this house. Lindy lives next door."

"A mighty barren existence. You got someone lookin' after you?"

"Of course you mean some *man.*"

"Yes, I do."

"We have each other. The two of us are enough."

"I like being alone, too," said Coburn. "But every now and then, it does a body good to lay eyes on other people. There's no one else here?"

Emma shook her head. "There was," she said. "There were twelve of us that founded the village." She nodded toward a yellow paper, a copy of the Homesteaders Act, framed and pinned to the wall. "I can show you all the government corners. We're here legal."

"Is there a name for this place?"

Emma gazed at the window. "We never could decide what to call it."

She was quiet for a time, and when he cleared his throat, she continued, more spirited. "When the others opted to move on, Lindy and I stayed."

She looked down at *The Tempest.* "Do you know the play?" she said.

Coburn shrugged. He liked to read, but he didn't always like talking about it. "More or less."

" 'My library was dukedom large enough,' " she quoted. "Act One, Scene Two." She tilted her chin again and looked down on him. "Can you understand that, Mr. Coburn?"

He swallowed the last of his coffee. Through the years, he'd known a lot of finely dressed folks, snobbish over money or power. But here was a woman living alone, clothed in little more than flour sacks and dust, more uppity than the lot of 'em.

"We're founders," said Emma, as if it explained everything there was.

If that don't beat all, thought Coburn.

Later, stretched out on the grass between the two houses, Coburn knew the peace he always felt under the stars. The storm had pulled in cool air welcome to both him and his horse who snored contentedly a few yards away. He closed his eyes, glad for the next day's work. He didn't understand people who loafed around all day, who would rather mew about like sick kittens. He liked working with his hands, liked riding and roping and doing all the things the world had shown him.

Danged if he understood these two fool women. When he threw down his bedroll on the lawn, Emma insisted that Lindy stay with her overnight in the bigger house, rather than retire to her own home. If the lady was half as smart as she thought she was, she would've known he had no designs on either of them. He just wanted to help folks out where he could, and then move on.

He drifted off thinking how he'd stack the timber. He came awake reaching for his gun, the buckskin stomping and snorting with concern.

"Hang on there, boy. Hang on," he said, not sure why he whispered, because the horse would wake the women well before his sleepy voice did.

Clank.

He heard something inside Lindy's vacant house. "Lindy?" he said into the darkness. "Emma?"

Once more the sound, and once more he called out. When no one answered, he carefully drew his revolver. A glance at the stars assured him it was still early.

"Come on out, now."

Nothing. Coburn could hear his heart beat, could feel the tingle in his arms, his legs. The iron in his hand was smooth, seductive in a way no woman could be. He liked this part of his life, too.

Another minute.

"Well, damn," he said.

With that, the door in the big house banged opened, and Emma scurried out with a kerosene lamp, the glow making his shadow tower across Lindy's place.

"Mr. Coburn? What is it?"

He didn't put his gun away, but answered without concern. "Nothing, ma'am. Probably some sort of critter." He smiled to himself. Figures that rabbit might show up now, while those rock biscuits and coffee roiled around his guts.

"Of course, there's no one here but us," said Emma.

He walked around the front step, peered into a window.

"It's just Lindy and me, here."

The lady's need to state the obvious tugged at Coburn's mood. She needed to go back inside.

Reassured, he walked back to the bedroll. "Most likely a rabbit," he said. "I'm going back to bed."

Emma stood on the porch holding the lamp for another few minutes. "There's no one here but us," she said, as she retired.

"Thought we was going to have an adventure," Coburn said aloud. When the horse didn't answer, he held his gun across his chest, closed his eyes and let himself doze, wondering who else lived in the settlement and why the women didn't want him to know.

If Lindy was more bashful at breakfast the next morning, her mother was equally less reserved. Keeping the air full of the hissing pop of eggs and wheat cakes, she jumped and bubbled like the bacon grease in her pan. For someone reluctant to accept his help the night before, today she had a full list of chores.

"After that, I really do think you should take a walk through Lindy's house, see if maybe somebody was in there last night. You might see something, anything, the kind of thing I wouldn't see in a million years."

"I doubt it," said Lindy. She brought her elbow to the table, dropped a lazy chin into her hand. "Don't bother yourself," she told Coburn

When he didn't answer, Emma asked again. "Will you look?"

Lindy sneered, poured herself some coffee.

Coburn promised he'd take a look. Then he said, "How far's your nearest neighbor?"

"There's the Calloway's about seven miles further west. And the Methodist tent village up north."

"How many there?"

"Oh, I have no idea," said Emma just a tick too quick. Her eyes never left her work as she cooked, her hands fumbling with the food. The woman was obviously no cook.

"They furnish the eggs?"

"Yes, a couple folks from there pass through here to trade."

"I can see what you get out of the deal," he said, frowning down at the smoking rubble on his plate. "But what do you give them?"

Emma turned with mock surprise. "Why, books of course. An education in the finer things of life."

"Ma's friend, Sam, likes Jane Austen," said Lindy with a derisive giggle. "I can't stand her."

"So you do have folks looking after you," said Coburn. He couldn't resist adding, " 'O brave new world! That has such people in it.' Act 5, Scene 1."

"You've been holding out on me, Mr. Coburn," said Emma. "You're more than you seem."

"I might say the same about you, ma'am. Who's this Sam fella?"

Emma scraped at the iron pan she held. "Have it your way, if you must," she said. "But we're not beholden to anyone."

"Still, you couldn't live here without them. Without Sam?"

"We make do." She let the pans clank together too loudly and wiped her slick hands on a stained cotton cloth. "Now it's time you got to work."

Coburn was glad to get back outside, away from the stifling smell in the house. He had sniffed a lot of pungent stuff through the years, from sick dogs and dead men to range riders whose idea of a regular toilet was crossing a stagnant crick during the annual cattle drive. This was like dry rot, only deeper, reaching clear to the soul.

During the morning he used an iron bar to pry apart twisted wood and further tear down the broken corral. Then he built up two piles, good wood and kindling.

He was almost done sorting through the debris when Lindy strolled out to the privy. On her way back to the house, she interrupted his work. "Why don't you like me?" she said.

He couldn't read her expression, wasn't sure what she was after. "Don't matter if I do or don't," he said.

"You ought to like me," she said. "I'm a founder." Again the word and an odd note of privilege.

"That ain't enough, Lindy," said Coburn. "I can't like you just for what you are."

"Of course you can."

"I like folks for what they do."

"I think you're a bore," she told him as she skipped away, and he grinned crookedly to himself.

By noon he had nearly finished repairs to the storage shack. He had accomplished much and enjoyed the satisfying trickle of sweat down his back. But the thought of lunch made him want to move on across the hills. The rested buckskin munched contently at a pan of dirty oats in the shade of Lindy's house, reminding him of his promise.

He'd drawn a pail of water that morning from the well, putting it close so the horse could drink. Now he downed a short tin as he stepped into Lindy's place.

The walls were unfinished, the floor nothing but packed dirt. A rough cedar chair and table sat against one wall. He walked on, letting his eyes adjust to the shade, not looking for anything, not sure what Emma wanted or didn't want him to see. He went through each of the three rooms twice. Before he left, he had a pretty good idea of what he'd heard the night before.

"Prairie dog," he told them over a meal of lard and molasses sandwiches.

"I haven't seen anything," said Emma. "Lindy hasn't mentioned it, have you Lindy?"

The girl wrapped a sticky strand of hair around her finger. "Never noticed," she said.

"Did you get rid of it?" said Emma.

"Never saw it," he said.

"Then," Emma said as she sat back, "how do you know it's a prairie dog?"

"Could tell by the leavings," he said. "Just like any critter." He held Lindy's gaze strong and steady while Emma began to clear the table. "You can tell what they are by what they leave behind."

That night he sat inside Lindy's house, pistol flat on the table, moonlight shading everything blue. He hated staying another night, but his conscience wouldn't let him leave. Coburn didn't like either one of the women, was pretty sure Emma was playing him, but he wasn't sure how. Things here were wrong, somehow, and he wanted to set them right. It's what he did. As his stomach churned, he knew one thing for certain — he wasn't sitting for any more of Emma's cooking.

Then just like the night before, the buckskin broke the silence with a nervous nickering. This time Coburn was wide awake, listening. In the next room, a soft rustling sounded, then a louder thump. Of the four windows in the place, three had glass, but the one facing the open range to the north was wide open. Someone had just invited themselves in.

"Your name Sam, by any chance?" said Coburn when the shadow rounded the corner. The figure whimpered, jumped back into the door jamb and fell over backwards.

"Take it easy, pardner." Coburn stood, the clumsy entrance causing him to let down his guard. The intruder charged at him, head down, scored a perpendicular hit to the stomach. Together the two hit the door and rolled into the yard. Coburn was up first. He stepped back and swung his leg out like a hayfork, lifting his adversary by the seat of the pants. The man went down, only to skitter backwards in the dirt like a crab and pull a knife from his belt.

Coburn sighed. Through the short exchange, he'd kept hold of his gun. Casually he pulled back the hammer. On the ground between them, he could see a book laying open in the moonlight. "Reckon you got a library card for that?"

"What is it, John?"

Coburn scratched at his neck, which had quickly gotten to be a habit when he heard Emma's voice. He couldn't recall her ever calling him by his first name.

"Library patron," he said. "Here to return a book."

Emma came to the porch holding the kerosene lamp high, Lindy at her side, neither of them showing any surprise at the nocturnal visitor.

"I've never seen him before in my life," said Emma. Lindy stood stoically, the ever present sneer at her lips. The visitor, on the other hand, was making all kinds of noise, but none of it resembled coherent speech. He shook his head, mumbled, looked from the gun to the women and back again.

"You're mute, aren't you?" said Coburn.

"He's trespassing," said Emma. "Breaking into my daughter's house. God knows what he planned to do."

"I reckon I know what Sam had planned." Keeping his gun level, Coburn reached into his pocket and pulled out a shiny belt buckle, tossed it on the ground. "Your name is Sam, isn't it?"

The man nodded.

"You left this behind last night," said Coburn. "No other reason I can imagine Lindy would have a man's belt buckle."

Nobody said anything, so Coburn stooped down for the book. *"Pride and Prejudice,"* he read. "That sums up the two of you real well."

"Are we going to stand here all night," said Emma, "or are you going to do something? Tell him . . ."

Coburn caught Emma glancing Sam's way for an instant, the look in her eyes hinting at sorrow and pain.

"Tell him to never come back."

When Sam didn't react to Emma's words, Coburn said, "That can be arranged." Still no reaction. "Not only can't Sam talk, he can't hear can he?"

"I don't know who this animal is, but it's up to you to protect us."

"You know your theater," said Coburn. "But you're a bad actor."

The wind blew cold.

"Which one of you girls has a boyfriend?"

Emma's wide eyes glowed red in the lamp light, while Lindy smiled, almost to herself.

"I'm not as well read as you, Emma," said Coburn with a broad grin. "But I know the old stories. Seems there's a sure fire way to wrap this up."

"I have no idea what you're talking about," said Emma.

Coburn pointed the gun at Sam, closed one eye, and pulled the trigger.

"Samuel!" cried Emma, heaving herself off the porch into the dirt. Falling to her knees, she crawled to Sam's side and cradled his head in her hands.

"Seems there was once two ol' girls fighting over a baby," said Coburn. "Both of 'em claimed ownership, but they agreed to let King Solomon decide. Solomon, being almost as wise as you, Emma, suggested they cut the child in half so it could be equally shared."

Sam sat up straight and returned Emma's embrace, while Lindy watched Coburn holster his gun.

"See, I think you and your ma both got a claim on this fella. But I also think she'd let him die rather than watch the two of you leave her here alone." For a few seconds, Coburn admired the bullet hole he'd put dead center through the water pail. Precisely where he'd wanted it to go. "At least that's what she thought."

Coburn sauntered casually past the couple on the ground and whistled for his horse. " 'The play's the thing,' " he quoted from a different book. With that, he led the buckskin out across the hills, wondering at the part he'd taken in Emma's drama, happy with the way it had played out.

LEONARD IN JAIL

With its head stuck inside a glass jar, the panic-stricken blue tabby ran straight into the dining room, crashing into Holt County Deputy Whit Branham's boot before rolling over into a table leg and springing up to run again.

Clara Byrnes wasn't far behind, her thick dark hair falling over her shoulders.

"Darn it, Whit, that cat's scratched me for the last time," but her voice held half a laugh, and genuine concern for the feline's well-being showed in her hazel brown eyes.

Branham pushed himself back from a half-eaten breakfast, hot ham and fried potatoes thick in his nose, hoping to cut off the cat's progress back toward the hotel's front desk.

The confused animal careened into an umbrella stand, half blind by the milky glass surrounding her face.

"Lizzy cat?" said Branham. "How in the world?"

"Canned beef," said Clara. "I emptied it this morning in the kitchen. She must've knocked it down off the counter."

Branham imagined the scene, pictured Lizzy, ever the curious feline, exploring the edges of a glass canning jar, licking at the fatty flavor, poking her head ever deeper into the jar until she was stuck.

"I'll get her," he said.

"She's really worked up. Don't get scratched," said Clara.

Dressed as he was in a long sleeved flannel shirt, denim trousers, and boots, Branham's protection was better than Clara's blue cotton dress and apron. He could wish for a pair of leather gloves, but there wasn't time.

"Give me that wool comforter from the back of the daybed," he said.

Clara nodded and pulled the thick embroidered quilt from the long stray-cushioned couch. She handed it across the table to Branham, knocking over his cup of coffee, staining the white linen cloth brown.

"I'll get that later," said Clara.

As Lizzy took a breather in the corner of the dining room between a walnut sideboard and the outside door, Branham gauged the distance between them and jumped.

Within seconds he had the squalling,

frightened cat wrapped in the quilt where her claws couldn't do any damage. After a minute or two, Lizzie quit struggling.

Under his rusty iron red mustache, Branham offered Clara a yellow-toothed smile.

"Now how do we get the jar off?" they both said at the same time.

"You hold the cat. I've got an idea," said Branham.

"Poor Lizzie. If we break the jar, we could get glass in her eyes."

"Only if we break it at the bottom. I'm gonna break it at the neck."

"Oh, I don't see how."

Branham had just the tool.

"Hold your horses," he said, leaving Clara with the wriggling bundle. He left the dining room, walked past the front desk and up the stairs to his bedroom.

The long steel fencing pinchers was in his tool box, right where he left it.

Back in the dining room, Clara sat on the floor with the quilt and cat in her lap.

"Don't hurt her, Whit."

"I got half a mind to knock her in the head," he said, "but no, I won't hurt her."

Branham knelt down, and careful not to put too much pressure on the cat's windpipe, he opened the pincher, edging one side of the head under the lip of the jar, between glass and fur.

Then Branham closed the pincher on the rim, crushing the glass, sending a crack down the length of the jar.

Lizzie jerked back and forth at the sound, and just when Branham thought Clara couldn't hold her, the glass split in two, one side rolling into the quilt, the other tumbling to the floor to break into three more pieces.

Standing up and stepping back fast, Clara let Lizzie jump to the floor where she rushed from the room shaking her head in fury.

Branham put the fencing pincher down next to his overturned cup.

"Hope she learns her lesson," said Clara.

"She won't. She's a stubborn one."

"She's lucky to have you living here." Clara's eyes darkened as they locked on Branham. "We both are."

"Hell, next time I'll let her suffocate."

Clara let her shoulder brush playfully against the deputy as she carried the quilt back to the daybed. "You don't fool me," she said. "I see the way you treat that dog of yours. You're a big old softie and your heart's bigger than the Nebraska prairie."

"Don't count on it," said Branham. His voice was gruff, but the smile was back. "Now where's my coffee?"

Clara stood with her hands on her hips, looking around, a puzzled expression on her face.

"Here's a better question. Where's Leonard?"

"What?"

"Speaking of your dog," said Clara. "Where is he? Where's Leonard?"

"Now that you mention it," Branham walked to the outside door and opened it onto the steep set of wooden stairs leading to the streets of O'Neill.

The landing was empty.

Branham had rolled out of bed at 5:30 and let his border collie, Leonard, out into the cool October darkness.

By the time Clara had breakfast ready, Leonard was usually scratching at the door.

He never missed a chance at table scraps.

"I'll be danged," said Branham. "He ain't here."

Leonard hated getting sidetracked.

That morning after the Branham Man opened the door for him, Leonard had quickly taken care of business in the dry brown grass between the hotel and the livery barn. Then, sniffing the south wind as he admired the orange crescent moon above the city's main street, he decided to head west and check out the hog pens at the Jacob House.

And half way there, a cotton-tailed rabbit had dared cut in front of him.

His salt and pepper muzzle twitched rapidly.

Not only did the rabbit cross his path, it had the nerve to stop dead in its tracks and let fly with the stinkiest stream of pee Leonard had ever sniffed.

There was no excuse for such a rude behavior.

A growl rolled up from under the white fur of his chest before he could stop it.

Twitching its ears at the warning, the rabbit froze.

Leonard crouched low, his own dark ears up, folding down at the tips. In the predawn darkness, with only a distant lantern inside the sheriff's office to add to the waxing moonlight, he didn't think the rabbit saw him.

But then, in a flurry of dust, it shot for a space between the mercantile and a parked buckboard wagon.

Again, Leonard couldn't stop the sounds that poured out of him. With a string of oaths, he bolted after the furry little offender.

The rabbit thought he was smart ducking

behind buildings and with a series of zigzags in the straight aways. What bunny boy didn't realize is that at the age of eight, Leonard had tasted his share of rabbit blood on the old chin.

Most of it cooked with gravy and potatoes by the Clara-lady.

And just like his master, he was an expert at running down low-life owlhoots.

By the time he and the rabbit reached the edge of town, Leonard had closed the distance between them by half. The critter still used the back and forth strategy, wasting time, losing ground.

Leonard laughed to himself even while unleashing another volley of fairly obscene language. "You don't stand a chance, rabbit."

And then just like that, with the eastern sky aglow and a few pastel pink clouds starting to take shape above the open range . . . his prey vanished.

Leonard slowed his pace to an easy lope. For the first time he noticed a steady stream of water, so he ran along the edge of a creek.

But which creek?

Where exactly had they ended up? And where was that rabbit?

Nose hard to the ground, he bulled forward, tail up and wagging.

Pig stink.

Yup! Pig Stink Creek.

Not far from the Jacob Hotel place. Another big house, like where he and Branham and Clara lived, where people stayed overnight.

Did the rabbit go into the creek?

Duck into a hole?

Leonard held his head high, his sparkling brown eyes catching the first rays of the new rising sun.

The pig stink lured him back east.

That's what he was after in the first place.

A hog slop breakfast had been his original goal.

Stupid rabbit.

He hated getting sidetracked.

And then another distraction.

Two men on horseback, one with a black beard carrying a boom stick high, the other hairless one with a person-pup on his lap, rode up and out of the creek.

The pup was squirming around in the hairless man's grip. Like he didn't want to go for a ride.

Leonard understood that.

He didn't like horses much either.

The man held his hand over the pup's mouth but as they turned toward main street, the young one cried out to Leonard.

Leonard barked a hearty "Good morning!" in reply.

The hairless man spun.

"Damn dog," he said.

Almost without warning, Blackbeard leveled the boom stick and set it off twice.

Just like Leonard knew all about rabbits, he knew about the sticks and the pain.

He was a law dog, after all.

He held his ground as two slugs tore up the sod on either side of him, missing.

The men gigged their horses forward and didn't look back as Leonard watched them go.

He walked over to where they'd climbed out of the crick, sniffed around and caught their scent.

Eventually, he wandered into town toward the Jacob House.

But by then the only thing on his mind was hog slop.

"Here comes that damn dog again," said Leroy Plugg, holding back the curtain, gazing out the window of his hotel room.

"Aw, leave it be," said Willy Tuck from where he sat on the bed. He stroked his long black beard and cursed. "Just leave it."

On the floor beside him, Willy's boy Albert played with a red ball and a handful of wooden blocks. Leroy watched as Albert built the blocks into a solid wall, then rolled the ball to knock it over.

"You know who that is?" said Leroy, wiping the sweat from his bald head "That's Whit Branham's dog. I thought I recognized it back at the crick, and now I'm sure of it."

"So what? Dogs wander all over this town."

"That dog's smart," said Leroy, looking back through the window, following the dog's progress until it trotted around the side of the building. "I'll bet you it knows what you and me are up to. I'll bet that dog tracked us here."

"It's a dog," said Willy. "Ain't no way it knows nothing about you and me."

"It's a deputy sheriff dog," said Leroy. "How do you know it ain't going to go back home to lead Branham here right now."

"And so what if he does?"

Albert had stacked up another wall of wood blocks. Happily, he rolled the ball and knocked the structure down.

At least the brat seemed happy now, had stopped bawling.

But Leroy's stomach still hurt, and he was sorry he'd agreed to help his friend carry the boy off.

"You 'spect your old lady is on our trail

by now?"

Willy shrugged. "Maybe," he said.

"She might go to Branham herself. Or to the sheriff. You said she saw you take him."

"Me and her is quits. Everybody knows it. I can say she's making up lies about me." Willy stood up beside the bed and walked to the window.

He jabbed a hard finger into Leroy's chest.

"Besides," he said, "she don't know you or where you live. You keep little Albert here for a few days, I'll walk around town in broad daylight, nobody will know the difference."

"What about Jacob? The man who runs the hotel?"

Willy rubbed his thumb and forefinger together. "I paid him plenty to keep quiet."

"What about that law dog?"

"Oh for cryin' out loud! I ain't worried about no damn dog."

"You oughtta be," said Leroy.

"Doggy?" said Albert.

"Don't you start now," Willy warned. He scratched the back of his head. "Look here. If it will make you feel better, I'll go outside right now and look around. If that dog is out there, I'll take care of it."

"How? How you gonna take care of it?"

Willy eyed the Winchester .30-.30 leaning

in the corner of the room under the accordion clothes rack.

"No sir," said Leroy. "You can't just walk out and shoot Whit Branham's dog in front of God and everybody."

Willy chewed the inside of his cheek. "You're probably right."

"You gotta be more careful. More tricky."

Willy walked back to the bed and pulled out a warbag from underneath.

"Lunch-lunch?" said Albert.

"No lunch-lunch," said Willy. "Not for you, boy." He reached into the bag and pulled out a strip of dry beef jerky. "But maybe lunch-lunch for that dog. What do you think of that Leroy?"

For the first time since all this nonsense began, Leroy smiled. "I think it's fine."

"You watch the kid."

Leonard kicked himself for being late.

He wasn't sure anymore what it was that kept him from getting to the hog pens earlier, but the breakfast stuff was already gone, devoured by the three grunting, squalling white fatties behind the cedar panel sty.

The three Jacobs pigs knew darn good and well that Leonard came past every morning.

You'd think they would've saved him a bite or two.

Nose to the fence, Leonard could smell potato skins, egg shells, bacon grease. All the good things that the Clara-lady kept in a bucket in the kitchen for her garden rather than toss to the hogs like the Jacob people did.

One of the pigs saw him and nudged the fence with its snout, letting go with a smelly belch just to rub things in.

Leonard didn't bother to growl at him.

Instead he turned and sniffed the air. It was time to get back home. Past time.

Sensing that he might be late, Leonard moved away from the pig pen, but curved back to the hotel in a big loop before he even realized what he was doing.

There, just inside the door to the privy where the hotel people did their business, a man stood holding a piece of meat.

Salty meat.

Spiced.

Salty.

Meat.

Leonard's ears went up and his wet black nose twitched.

It might be deer meat, he thought. Smelled like deer.

He walked straight ahead, grateful that

somebody was willing to share some break-fast.

Then he stopped, catching another scent.

And Leonard remembered.

It was the beard man. The one with the boom stick from that morning.

He started to growl, but stifled it.

Dumb.

No man fed a growling dog.

If he wanted the meat, he'd have to be friendly.

Besides, the bearded man didn't have the gun anymore.

Wagging and ignoring his initial sense of caution, Leonard stepped up to the door.

The man tossed the meat inside.

Leonard walked in and grabbed the strip of meat between his teeth.

He was right.

It was deer!

Too late, he realized he'd been tricked, and the bearded man slammed the door on him, locking Leonard in jail.

He felt pretty stupid.

But tasting the deer jerky on his lips was worth it.

Spending the morning fixing an axel on the hotel's wagon made a man hungry, and Branham was half way through his second helping of pork fritters before he looked up and said, "Leonard ever come home?"

With a stack of dishes in her hands, Clara followed out two hotel guests. "Don't believe so," she called back.

"Huh," said Branham, shoveling in a forkful of cooked cabbage.

Across the table, a man dressed in a white shirt and black hammer-claw tailed jacket smiled. "Who's Leonard?" he said.

"Dog," said Branham.

"How long's he been missing?"

Branham stopped chewing and looked thoughtfully at the man. "He ain't exactly missing."

"But he hasn't come home?"

"No. He hasn't."

The man struck a match on his boot and lit a cheroot. Holding it between two fingers he pulled in a lungful of smoke. As he exhaled, he smiled.

"He was my dog, I might go out and look for him."

Rather than be angry at the man for the unsolicited advice, Branham thought about his and Clara's morning adventure with Lizzie the cat and felt guilty.

What if Leonard was in trouble?

What if, like Lizzie the cat, he had his head stuck in a jar somewhere? What if he wanted to come home but couldn't?

Branham wiped his face with a cloth napkin and tossed it over the uneaten food on his plate. Then he grabbed his hat from the floor next to his chair.

Abruptly standing, he nodded at the man. "I'm obliged to you," he said.

The man nodded back through a swirl of smoke.

Outside, Branham slapped his hat to his head and pounded down the steps. It wouldn't do to go calling out loud and draw attention to himself.

Then he thought about Lizzie again and let out a loud, "Leonaaaaardd!"

Noon on main street and busy as it was with horses, wagons, and pedestrians, there wasn't a dog to be seen. "Leonard!" he called again.

Where could he be?

Ever since Branham had rescued the dog from a barbed-wire fence more than a year before, Leonard had been a loyal companion.

And fairly predictable.

In fact, he was nothing if not predictable.

Every morning he did his job in the grass, then circled over to the Jacob House hog sty. Old man Jacob never said a word, and Branham figured the hotelier was too hung over most mornings to notice.

Still, if there was a chance the old boy had seen Leonard that morning, he'd take it.

Trying not to be rude, Branham hurried down the street and across the boardwalks, tipping his hat to the ladies and waving at men he knew on the street. Twice his friends tried to stop him with chatter, and twice Branham shook his head, indicating with his firm eyes that he was on official business.

That's about the time he realized he wasn't carrying a gun.

To rescue Lizzie, he needed a wire pinchers.

Who knows what kind of trouble Leonard was in?

He almost turned back, but shrugged inwardly.

Why would he need a gun?

When he found out what kind of fix the dog was in, he'd just have to improvise.

If he found out.

Out on the open range, animals sometimes just disappeared. Even the most loyal.

Putting thoughts like that out of his mind, Branham tromped forward.

From the boardwalk in front of the Frontier newspaper office, he crossed the street toward the Jacob House.

The Jacob House hotel was longer than Clara's place, and not as wide. While it did have two upstairs rooms, the rest were on the ground floor. Out back was a small lean-to style building for boarding a few horses, Leonard's favorite hog-pen, and a privy.

Above him, two pair of eyes, watched him with mixtures of surprise and contempt.

"Dammit, I told you," said Leroy. "I told you that dog would lead Branham straight to us. I thought you said you took care of that mutt?"

"I did," said Willy. "Ain't no way he got out where I locked him."

"Well, somebody must've let him out."

"I wedged the door shut," said Willy. "Take a mighty strong man to pry it open."

"So how do you explain Branham coming here? Coming straight for us?"

Willy looked at Leroy, then turned back to stare at Albert sleeping on the bed.

"I can't," he said.

"Grab the kid," said Leroy. "We'll make a run for it."

Behind the hotel, the dark inside of the privy was getting hot.

Coupled with the buzzing of flies and heady aromas, Leonard was more than a little bit annoyed.

Usually the smell of a good old latrine appealed to Leonard's basic instincts.

But not when he was a prisoner.

It was like he was in jail!

After swallowing his meaty snack and licking his lips, he realized the Jerky Man had closed the door behind him.

Rude, he thought, but typical. People were always closing the privy doors.

In fact, they were closed more open than not.

But then Leonard tried to paw the door open.

Finding it stuck fast, he started to have suspicions about the Jerky Man.

Maybe it was more than being rude. Maybe he'd played a trick on Leonard.

The dog stood up on his hind legs and fell against the inside of the door, scraping frantically with his paws over and over.

No good.

Sitting in the silent darkness, meditating on his options, Leonard decided the only thing he could do was bark.

It certainly wasn't his first choice. He was, after all, a self-sufficient beast.

But, he thought to himself, sometimes even the best of us need to call for help.

He started to bark.

And once he started, he realized it was meditative for him. All his anxieties at being locked in stayed firmly at bay as long as he could shout and yell and curse about his predicament.

He barked, he whinnied, he scraped at the door with his paws.

He even let out a good yowl.

Then he barked some more. And more after that.

And just like he'd expected, the door popped open and the Branham Man was there.

What took you so long? thought Leonard.

But then, overcome with gratitude, he jumped at the deputy, giving him a couple licks on the hand in thanks.

"I thought that was you carrying on," said Branham. "How'd you get in there."

"Don't move, Branham," said a low voice.

Branham put his hands up and turned around slow, letting Leonard prance out to the side, ears at attention.

"Stay, boy," he said, and Leonard more or less obeyed, passing back and forth between the lawman and the privy.

"That's a pretty good dog you got, leading you right to us."

Branham had no idea what the big man with the black beard was talking about. But since he held the rifle, and since it was pointed straight at Branham's chest, he decided not to argue.

"Ain't no need for gunplay," he said.

"You coming, Leroy?" the bearded man called over his shoulder.

"I'm comin', I'm coming," said a second man, hurrying out of the back door of the hotel with a wiggling boy strapped under one arm, the kid looked to be two or three, and when the sunlight hit him he started to bawl.

"Shut up, Albert," said Willy, bouncing up and down as he ran along. "Don't just stand there, Willy, get us some horses."

Willy, the bearded one, turned his attention away from Branham for a split second.

But it's all the time the deputy needed.

Snapping his fingers at Leonard, he clucked his tongue. "Go, boy," he said, and Leonard took off like his feet were on fire.

It was the kind of day a dog lived for, thought Branham, with no way to know how close the dog's thoughts echoed his own.

The Jerky Man, the one with the beard, who'd been rude enough to trick him, was now the one pointing a boom stick at Leonard's friend.

Immediately remembering the morning scene at the creek, Leonard knew the owlhoot wouldn't be afraid to pull the bang switch. Leonard had no intention of giving him that chance.

The growl came up from his chest, unbidden, but welcome.

Within seconds of Branham's command, Leonard had the Jerky Man on the ground, the dropped rifle well out of reach, his bared fangs only inches from the man's puckered face.

Just for fun, while Branham took care of the other man, Leonard let a long stream of drool fall onto his victim's beard.

"You spoil that dog too much," said Clara from her place on the daybed, Lizzie the cat curled up on her shoulder, nesting in her hair.

"You have no room to say a word," said Branham as he shoveled a helping of beef post roast and gravy onto a plate.

Setting it down carefully to the hotel floor, he gave the dog a familiar scratch behind the ears. Leonard winked at Branham with appreciation, then attacked the plate with gusto.

"At the very least, he's a lucky dog," said Clara. "Though I might admit you're the lucky one for having him."

"And that's one sentiment I won't say a

word against," said Branham. "I wouldn't argue that at all."

The Ballad of Dorothy Kotraba

1973

Grandma's friend Rose dropped four heaping teaspoons of Sanka into a chipped glass mug before dumping in some boiling water to stir. An acrid froth formed as she worked a spoon through the brew before sliding it my way. Letting it cool, I sawed out a chunk of frozen boxed pie, the kind with a half-life measured in geological years.

We were at Rose's house to look at old photos, her hope being that Grandma could identify the increasing number of faces Rose didn't remember. The two octogenarians were only a few years apart in age, had grown up together in the same Lutheran church. Closer than sisters, they often finished each other's sentences. For the first half hour they talked about historic family trips, Sunday picnics, and Lawrence Welk, who played at the local dance pavilion when they were young.

When the topic finally turned to scrapbooks, Rose went to her bedroom and carried out a torn cardboard box with photos and loose newspaper clippings sliding around inside. Plopping it onto the couch in the living room, she invited us in.

"What's this?" I said, holding up a thin five-by-seven paperboard book.

"That, my dear, is an autograph album," said Rose. "It belonged to my mother."

The pages were brittle and yellow, each one dated more than ninety years before, each inscribed with some sort of verse or brief homily. I read the entry by Alfred Jones aloud:

A place for my name in your album,
a place for my name in your heart,
a place for us both is in heaven,
where good friends do never part.

"Sort of morbid," I said, but Grandma laughed. As the two ladies chattered along, I read another:

I wish you health and happiness
I wish you gold in store
I wish you heaven after death
What could I wish you more?

More heaven. More death. "What was

with these people?"

"I don't suppose teenage girls have changed much over the years," said Rose. "Drama and dark, happiness and light. Fantasy and grandiose schemes."

Grandma agreed and complimented Rose on the pie.

Then something at the back of the book caught my eye. While all of the other missives were in pencil, this one had been written in pen. Big and bold in jet black ink, unaffected by time. Whoever wrote it had used a strong hand.

I read the entry, disbelieving; read it again.

"Who is Dorothy Ann Kotraba?" I asked. Both women fell silent, suddenly preoccupied with the lint in the carpet and loose threads on their skirts.

"Shall I heat your coffee?" said Rose, and Grandma nodded vaguely.

What had I said? The name obviously had an effect on their good mood, probably with good reason. There was no mistaking the friendship for Rose's mother that Dorothy had put into the four lines. There was no mistaking the tone of voice, a self-confidence missing from the other pages.

Wilma is your name
Innocent is your station

I'll put in the ground the son of a gun
who makes the alteration.

"She must have been some character, whoever she was," I said.

"She was a Czech," said Rose with strong disdain. "Older than my mother by several years."

"She was a one room school teacher," said Grandma brightly, but Rose scowled anyway.

"Let me get you some more coffee," she said, though my cup was still full.

1873

Seventeen weeks on a boat. Seventeen weeks sick with rancid food and water. And that was after the turmoil of getting permission to leave Suchdol in the southern part of the Empire. The long walk to the coast with its endless series of checkpoints, and Otek Kotraba, her father, losing the irreplaceable Reise Pass more than once.

And now this. Dorothy stood in shadow at the top of the hotel stairway and pushed her corset up, straightening the slim skirt, wiggling around in the garter and stockings. The clothes were uncomfortable, and stuffing her buxom frame into the lacy unmentionables had seemed like a waste of time.

She puffed out her cheeks and blew out with disgust. The men liked it. It added spice to the transaction. A flour sack dress wouldn't put food on her table.

Fortunate enough to find space on the boat, she and her father had arrived in America with little more than their dreams intact. But hadn't her cousin Thomas built those dreams into magnificent towers? His letters from the frontier had been more than encouraging. In the new town of Red Horizon, just across the muddy river in the young state of Nebraska, there would be land and freedom.

After less than a year in the fledgling settlement, Tom's dream towers proved unreal. Dorothy taught at the one-room school house, but when locusts razed the Kotrabas' first crop and fire took their house, she and Otek went back to Sioux City to find any work they could, hoping to save enough to stake a new beginning — not just for them, but for Thomas, his wife and two children, too. Dorothy worked days in a laundry. Her father worked nights in a candle factory.

But it was with a regular room at the Franklin Hotel that she made more money than both jobs combined. Her father didn't know about that.

Lamplight flickered across the stairway's brown wallpaper, bringing the floral patterns there to rhythmic life. Dorothy kept her breathing as slow as she could, but her heart was quick in her chest. She was just twenty years old, but the job made her feel older and, though she prayed for forgiveness, more alive. This wonderful, terrible new job. In the Old Country, who would have dreamed such a thing?

"I'm afraid I have to call it a night, gentleman," said the fat man seated below. Dorothy admired his expensive black suit, clean and pressed, his curly white hair, neatly clipped. Her slim, cool hand lightly dancing on the polished wood railing, she eased down the steps to get a better view of the table.

The fat man sat with his back to Dorothy and the staircase, arms stretched out greedily, paper money and gold coins in his embrace. Facing him sat two scar-faced cowboys, not much older than Dorothy, hard men who reminded her of the settlers she'd met in Nebraska.

"Ain't sure you played them hands square, Mr. Lamb," said one of the drovers, his voice thick with an Irish accent.

"Course we got no proof," said the other as they both stood, while Lamb gathered up his deck of playing cards.

"When luck is in charge of the game, who's to say what's fair?" said Lamb, stowing the deck in a side pocket of his jacket. "I'll thank you to be good sports about this."

Lamb slid back and lifted himself up with great effort. "Here," he said, tossing each of his opponents a gold piece. "Have a drink . . . and a bath on me."

Neither one of the men accepted the peace offering, turning instead toward the open door of the hotel lobby. While Lamb raked in his winnings, one of the men carefully built a smoke before both of them sauntered into the late summer night.

Dorothy admired the stack of coins Lamb was counting, lantern light skimming the curved edges like lines of liquid fire. There was a lot of money there, but she had at least that much tucked away in a sack at the boarding house where she and her father stayed. Her breathing picked up. She smoothed back her hair, leaned across the banister and shoved her chest directly toward Lamb. Tonight, if all went well, she could double her stash.

"I'm happy you won your poker game," she said.

Lamb turned, looked up with his shiny red face, his neat white mustache. "Am I late for our appointment, Dot?" His smile was wide, but something in his voice betrayed a dark mood. She reminded herself that having only met Lamb a few hours before, she didn't know the man well at all. She told herself to be careful.

"No," said Dorothy. "You're not late at all." Her English was good, better than her father's, but still she was deliberate with her words. She made her way down the stairs, enticing, but not overly temptuous. Warm, but not loving.

Their transaction was hardly about love.

She had heard about Joshua Lamb a week before. The man was over from Chicago, hoping to capitalize on property in Sioux City, maybe back a settlement of his own in the rich farm land west of the river. People said he liked to eat, play cards, and spend money like crazy. In the hotel lobby, Dorothy had watched him do all three. She had heard he liked other things, too.

"Join me for a drink before we go up?" he said, pulling irritably at the string tie around his neck, partially exposing the sweaty flesh beneath his white shirt.

She put her arms around him and pressed close. Slowly, she moved her fingers up his body, walking her left hand to his thick neck, letting her right hand roam across his jacket. She untied his tie and, removing it, pushed it into his pocket.

"I need to use the privy," she said. "I'll meet you."

"God's blood, woman, but you are a peach," he said.

1973

In the Diamond Jubilee book, Dorothy posed with the 1905 Lutheran Church Ladies Aid in a wooden kitchen with a big wood stove behind them. I wondered if she thought much about the land she'd left behind, her youth, its hardships. The picture showed a heavy set woman of the times, with gray hair and wire-rimmed glasses. Dorothy hardly seemed menacing in middle age.

"There were so many stories about her," said Rose. "Things nobody wanted to talk about."

"But apparently did," I said, a comment which got a smile out of both women.

Grandma planted her index finger on the page in front of me.

"There's a lot of history here. Germans, Swedes, Czechs. But it's not all written down."

"And maybe it shouldn't be," said Rose. "Plenty folks built this country on honest work. No sense going on about them that didn't."

I was puzzled by her attitude. "It says here that Dorothy taught school all over the county until her retirement in 1910."

"She had a job on the side," said Rose. "It started in Sioux City, but she brought it back to Nebraska like a disease. Carried on the entire time she taught."

"What kind of job?"

I didn't get an answer.

1873

Dorothy's room was at the back of the hotel, looking out onto an alley filled with garbage. It didn't matter. She was never there in the daytime to see it. But the season was still unbearably hot, so she kept the window open despite the smell and animal sounds.

She had done nothing to personalize the place. At the back of her door, she had a wooden hanger with a few light unmentionables, a mirror on the wall over the bed. A small shiver ran through Dorothy when she saw herself in the glass.

"Shall we do the payment first, dear?" said Lamb, his breath laced with whiskey, his bulk filling half the space.

Dorothy swallowed hard, walked to the

bed, lifted her skirt. The truth was she had only done this a few times before, and that was with local boys who had more money than sense. But she had to start somewhere. She needed the client list. She needed the inventory.

Hiking her leg onto the bed, garter exposed, she pulled a wad of bills from the top of her stocking and handed it over.

Lamb was a high roller, a big man with connections to other big men. Dorothy coveted men like him. His secret trade represented salvation, because Dorothy wasn't selling. She was buying.

Lamb picked up the candle and walked to the window. Drawing back the curtain, he lifted the flame, a signal for the men waiting. In the thick dusk, she watched as they pulled a long wooden trunk from their wagon and carried it to the back entrance. The night was quiet. Before long, they were coming up the steps, working hard, groaning with their burden.

Once they entered the room, Lamb dismissed the men. They left the big wooden trunk sit in the middle of the room. When Lamb lifted the lid, Dorothy saw a dozen new army rifles and enough cartridges for them all.

"I can have another dozen for you next

month," he said. "After that, I don't know."

"I have these as good as sold," she told him. "What I really need is revolvers."

Her eyes held the question, and he nodded. "By God you're a peach," he smiled, but there was no joy in his brief laughter. "But if we go too fast, we'll both end up in a federal prison."

He helped her shove the box under the bed. "Any trouble with the locals?"

"None," she lied. Long as she kept her inventory safe, she told herself, she'd be okay.

"Now what say we consummate the deal?" said Lamb, his voice low and purring. "I didn't climb all them stairs just for business."

Dorothy's eyes darted around the room. Naturally, she had expected the advance. Playing the harlot convincingly in the lobby below, it had happened before.

"That isn't part of the deal," she said.

But she hadn't counted on the fat man's quick reflexes. As she brought the Army Colt up from under her pillow, he struck out with a closed fist, knocking her backwards. The gun landed flat on the floor, but thankfully didn't go off. Lamb was literally panting, his stubby tongue flicking at the corners of his mouth.

"You don't want to do this, Mr. Lamb," she said.

His eyes took on a malicious glaze as he clomped toward her in the dim candle light. A light breeze came through the open window. Lamb reached for his belt. "Oh, but I do," he hissed.

Dorothy turned to the window, calling out with the sound of a morning dove, a song uncanny in the city's dark night. Stranger still, her call was almost immediately answered.

When she turned back to the room, Lamb was upon her, taking both her wrists in one gaping paw, pushing her onto the bed. Pinned under his bloated weight, there was nothing she could do. He said something unrecognizable, grunted heavily, and hooked his free hand into the front of her blouse.

Dorothy closed her eyes and thought about the trunk under her bed, about the guns she had bought and sold during the past few weeks, and the cash she'd tucked away for her family. Rigid now in Lamb's sweaty grasp, she wondered if it had all been worth it.

Above her, Lamb was still. The stink of his breath was on her, but he had stopped moving. She squirmed roughly, and the grip on her wrists relaxed.

"That's no way to treat a lady," said the Irish cowboy, the barrel of his six shooter buried in the fold at the back of Lamb's neck. "On your feet, Lamb."

As if preparing for another game of cards, Lamb stood slowly and smoothed out the wrinkles in his coat, brushed his trousers and cleared his throat. Slowly he turned to face the two scar-faced drovers from before. Irish kept his gun trained on the fat man, while the other cowboy held up Lamb's deck of cards.

"Gentlemen," whispered Lamb. "Looks as though my luck has turned."

"Cards are marked," Irish said. "Kind of like we figured."

Dorothy smiled to herself as she recalled her antics in the lobby, pushing Lamb's tie away while palming the deck of marked cards from his jacket. Cards she had delivered to the cowboys when pretending to visit the outhouse.

"We'll all be leaving you alone now, ma'am," said Irish, nodding his head.

As she watched the cowboys lead Lamb from the hotel, she let her mind drift to a time when she would have enough of a stake to go back to Red Horizon, maybe teach school again. Maybe she would keep her business going. The polished carbines in the trunk called to her.

She laughed to think about it. A proper school teacher. An arms dealer. If the children found her stock, she'd tell them she was afraid of the Indians.

1973

During the centennial celebration, Grandma, Rose and I watched Dorothy Kotraba's granddaughter Maggie give a speech about the early days of the Czech settlers and the struggles they overcame. The crowd snoozed.

Maggie finished up by sharing Dorothy's secret family recipe for mulberry kolaches, an old country jelly roll. The crowd clapped politely. Mayor Smith gave Maggie a press-board plaque with an engraved square of foil commemorating her family and its rock solid place in a community founded on neighborly love, heavenly virtue, and commitment to the principles of American free enterprise. Something, he said, Dorothy would be proud of.

Last Day at Red Horizon

Red Horizon was a splintered ruin. Not a clapboard building stood untouched, not a hitching post unmoved. If John Coburn was losing his mind, then the buckskin he rode was loco too as it shied from the field of rubble. How could so much have changed in only eight years?

The confluence of the Missouri and Niobrara Rivers was an ideal place for the booming settlement of determined farmers and merchants, but while Coburn had been working cattle in Wyoming, his home town had gone away like powder smoke, leaving in its place a wasteland of torn prairie and splintered wood skeletons.

He rubbed his eyes. The false front of Mill's General Store listed earthward; the smith's shop had only two walls. The rest of the buildings were the same — broken, like a boy's set of blocks kicked over and partly buried in the yellow fescue and sod.

It was late October, and the afternoon sky was a deep blue glaze. "Go," he said, and the horse moved ahead. Coburn held his fleece-lined coat tight to his neck, and the long hem pulled at the weight of his gun belt. Flint gray eyes studied the chaos, searching for an explanation. What the hell had gone on?

A cold wind blew spinning cottonwood leaves around the valley, kicking up dust on faint grid lines, abandoned roads almost completely reclaimed by nature. A jackrabbit skittered sideways to the west, then ducked backward to vanish behind a roll of earth. This land could trick a man, seeming flat while hiding countless hills and hollows.

Coburn steered the horse around the abandoned town along the bank of Dirk's Crick, crossed over on a bed of mud and leaves, then pushed uphill through 100 yards of brome. He rode past the one-room schoolhouse, still intact, into a belt of tangled cedars behind where the livery stable should have been. On the other side of the trees, Coburn sat tall and peered across three miles of dry yellow grassland, the crick line gray and blurring in the distance where it eventually fed the Niobrara.

Just as he caught sight of the congregational church steeple to his right, someone said, "Get down nice and slow, stranger. Or I'll kill you dead as a rock."

Coburn took his hands from the horse's dark mane and, whispering calm words in its ear, remained still. He turned his head a fraction and the voice came again.

"I swear to God, mister."

"I'm not in the habit of taking orders," he said. For all he knew, the old coyote was armed with a busted cedar bough.

When the man didn't answer, Coburn counted his options. Make a quick break? Gallop away? Turn fast and fight? The buckskin was up to it, and he pulled his Colt faster than most. Still, if the man had a scattergun, he could lose the horse easy enough, if not his own life. Plus there was the mystery of the town to study on. Something had happened to the people, his people, and Coburn wagered his assailant had some answers. He swung down gracefully and touched ground.

A fat devil with a wooden tooth, brown shirt, and long dark vest emerged from the woods with a 12-gauge leveled at Coburn's chest. High up, almost on his shoulder, he wore a dirty silver star. "That's fine," said the man. "Now toss down your gun."

"I don't have a gun," Coburn lied. His

coat fell just short of his knees, heavy and covering his belt.

"Pretend you do," said the man. "Toss it down."

Coburn weighed his next move. Curiosity, more than anything else, forced the decision. His arm was molasses rolling under the coat, separating iron from leather, taking all day to do it. Finally, the gun fell to earth. Keeping the shotgun at waist level, the fat man scooped up the six-shooter and waved it triumphantly.

"My name's Silas Brahm," he said. "Tell me yours, and we'll have a drink."

"Name's John Coburn."

Brahm smiled and shifted the wooden tooth in its socket. "Glory be," he said mockingly, "if it ain't him what's called The Peregrine."

With freshly whitewashed walls and a foundation of dark wooden beams, the congregational church was in fairly good repair, though part of the floor was gone. Most of the pews were missing too, but the original carved walnut altar rested at the far wall. Wooden crates covered with blankets were stacked against the west wall, and Coburn recognized furniture from the Red Horizon Hotel and tables from the saloon.

"Where is everyone?" asked Coburn.

"Gone." Brahm motioned to follow him. "Gone to meet their maker. Some of them."

"The others?"

"They're gone too. Here and there." Brahm waved the shotgun high and to the west. "Now sit down."

"I'd like some answers, mister —"

"Sheriff," said Brahm, indicating a pair of chairs on either side of a table.

"Sheriff," said Coburn. "I grew up here, had friends and kin."

"We all lost folks, Mr. Peregrine," said Brahm.

"Let's have that drink."

"Yeah, let's do that."

Brahm leaned his gun against the wall before unloading Coburn's Colt, absently dropping the lead into his shirt pocket.

"I'm sorry about the gun," said Brahm. "But, I'm still the law here." He grabbed a bottle from a shelf. "Whiskey?"

Coburn nodded.

Brahm brought two glasses to the table and planted a bottle between them. "I still ain't sure you're not hiding more weapons from me." He poured a measure for each of them and slid one forward while swallowing the other. "A knife, maybe?" He coughed.

In Wyoming, Coburn made a name for

himself with the six-inch throwing dagger he kept in his boot — a gift from Standing Bear's son and his most cherished possession. Either Red Horizon had heard a few stories about its prodigal son or Brahm was a good guesser — maybe both.

"Doesn't matter," said Brahm. "You keep it."

Coburn sipped his whiskey in silence while the fat man cleared his throat.

"I heard of you," Brahm said. "How men call you The Peregrine because you wander far and wide." He flapped his hands like wings. "Flying off here or there. Heard you was in Cheyenne a while back." His smile waned. "I should tell you about your family." He poured another drink. "Didn't know your mother."

"She died in childbirth," said Coburn. "I never knew her myself."

"I came here from Chicago much later, in '79, two years before that damnable winter," said Brahms.

A damnable winter it had been. In the first months of 1881, ill-prepared homesteaders and pioneers on the high plains were hit with wind and snow that seemed almost supernatural in origin. No one could imagine anything worse than the endless days of gray skies and ice, until spring came with a fresh and more relentless pair of hells.

"When the flood came, nobody did more than your pa." Brahm swallowed his drink and said, "He was a good man. But then the sickness came too. By August he had the fever. A week later, he was gone. Your sister died too. Lots more folks."

Coburn stood and walked to the door, a tightness growing in his chest. He and his father had never been close, but his feelings for Rachel, his younger sister, ran deep. Even now there were gifts for her in his saddlebag, gifts she'd never see. Or so he was being told.

"It's only been a few years. Surely 200 people weren't all lost to fever and flood." said Coburn.

"A handful remained. The last ones headed for higher ground this past spring."

"Then why are the buildings torn to hell? The damage here looks more like the result of dynamite than flood." Coburn glanced again at the pile of wooden crates.

Brahm stood and rounded the table. "Plenty of time to show you. Have another drink."

"You say you knew my family," said Coburn. "I'd like my gun back."

"Maybe," said Brahm. "After I ask you a couple more questions."

Coburn turned his back and leaned on the doorframe. "I'm the one should be asking questions."

"What do you know about the hold up of a stagecoach here in 1880?" said Brahm.

"Nothing."

"Came out of Yankton, carrying mail. Turns out it also had several thousand dollars in gold coins and jewelry."

"Why ask me about it?"

Brahm sucked at his wooden tooth and spit on the floor. "Three men, masked, took the money at gunpoint. And knife point. Shotgun rider on the stage took a throwing dagger to the chest."

"And the driver?"

"Dead too, shot through the neck."

"You got something to say, say it."

"Thing is, the hold-up men just up and vanished. No one saw them leave town."

"Are you saying they stayed here?" said Coburn. "Hid out in plain sight?"

"Before long, there were stories about how they split the take and each man hid his share here, then rode out later." Brahm lowered his voice. "Was you one of them three men, Peregrine?"

Coburn turned. "I'd like my gun back, Sheriff."

"Maybe you could show me where you

hid your share?"

"Point me in the direction of those last town folk so I can head after them."

"No sir," said Brahm. "You better think about what I said. Then, when you're ready to confess," he held his hands out and chuckled, "then we'll make us a deal."

Coburn took a step toward Brahm, felt the back of his skull cave in, and for a long time saw only darkness.

A heavy ball of pain rolling inside his head forced Coburn to open his eyes to daylight streaming through a window with three iron bars. Everything about the previous day was a kaleidoscope of mixed images. He tried to stand but met immediate resistance, and he fell back against a rusty iron framework. His wrists were bound at floor level with what felt like a leather bridle strap.

"Whoa there, friend. Take it easy, now." The elderly voice came from across the room. Coburn made out the shadow of a fellow prisoner, his arms also bound from behind. "We ain't going nowhere," said the prisoner.

"Who are you?"

"Name's William Carson. Call me Bill."

"Why . . . ?"

"Why are we here? Well, that's easy."

Carson tried unsuccessfully to shrug, and Coburn saw the other man was tied to the iron frame of a cushionless cot. "We both came in on the middle of some underhanded shenanigans."

"Don't understand." The throbbing pain in Coburn's head made it hard to focus.

"Silas Brahm ain't who he claims to be," said Carson.

"Sheriff?"

"Just the opposite, son. He's Jacob Finch. He robbed the Yankton stage with Eli Faraday."

Whiskey and talk of his sister's death had distracted him. Coburn cursed himself for being caught off guard.

"Finch said my sister died, that the valley flooded."

"Red Horizon flooded, alright. There was stories as far south as Omaha about the sickness and ague."

"You from Omaha?"

"Deputy federal marshal," said Carson. "I been looking for these boys a long time."

"I knew it wasn't just flood water that ripped apart the buildings."

"He's got a dozen crates of dynamite. Surely been doing some damage." Carson paused. "He got the drop on me when I rode through those cedars behind the church."

"That's where he got me," said Coburn.

"He had another man with him," said Carson. "He's got a new partner."

"Not Faraday?"

"Faraday died in Wyoming. On his deathbed, he gave up Finch and admitted to hiding the loot in Red Horizon."

Coburn closed his eyes and thought about the dynamite, the broken buildings.

"Naturally," Carson said, "Faraday didn't say exactly where he'd hidden his share."

"And Finch doesn't know where it is."

"That's right. He's going crazy trying to find it, and not being too careful about the hunt, I might add."

"There's something else he's not too careful about," said Coburn, leaning back into the jail cell door, prying at his right boot with his left toe until the leather slipped. "He knows me, knows I carry a knife." He shucked his foot from the boot, and the blade slid to the floor within reach of his leg.

"He wants us to escape," said Carson.

Bending his knee, Coburn pulled the knife as close as he could, then used the weight of his body to drag it along the floor under him and back toward his hands. The pain in his head had ballooned, but he got the hilt within reach of his fingertips.

"He knows I've been out west. Maybe thinks I crossed paths with Faraday and came home to pick up his share."

"He's hoping you'll lead him to it," said Carson.

Coburn had the knife between two of his fingers and struggled to slice the tight bonds. In less than five minutes, the job was done. Within minutes, the older man's bonds were cut too, and together they moved to the jail cell door.

"Look at this." Carson slid back a single bolt and swung the door wide. "It wasn't even locked."

Coburn's eyes scanned the interior of the wood frame building. The front door faced open prairie toward the crick and a roundabout leading up the cedar trail.

"He'll be watching," said Carson. "Don't forget his partner."

"Doesn't matter. Wherever we go, Finch is sure to follow."

The fresh autumn air cleared his head, and Coburn set his sights on the town's one-room school house, climbing the trail with Carson on his heels.

"Do you have a plan, John?" said Carson.

"Yep," said Coburn. "I'm going to lead him to Faraday's gold."

■ ■ ■ ■

"What's our move here, John?"

Carson stood in the doorway while Coburn moved through the long rows of seats. A blackboard stood in the corner, and the teacher's desk was tipped over backwards, its emptied drawers scattered all around.

Finch had been here, tossing the obvious hiding places, ignoring those he wasn't aware of.

"I came here from the time I was seven until I was twelve," Coburn said. "Teacher's name was Dorothy Ann Kotraba, a sweet old Bohemian."

Carson stepped into the room. "Finch'll be here soon," he said.

"You're right," said Coburn. He looked around the room before closing his eyes and breathing deep. "I can still smell the chalk dust, still hear the girls in the seats behind me giggling. They were twins from a German famfly."

"Who cares? I'd like to know what you're going to do when Finch gets here."

"You know what made Red Horizon special, Marshal? All the families that settled here from all the different countries. It was a melting pot all by itself." Coburn smiled.

"Close your eyes, Carson. You can smell the history."

The old man reluctantly complied. "Do you actually know where Faraday hid his share of the gold?" he said.

"As a matter of fact," said Coburn. "I do."

Carson opened his eyes, and The Peregrine was gone.

The old man met Finch at the door, the fat man panting from the steep incline to the school.

"Where is he?"

"Not sure," said Carson. "He was here just a minute ago."

"If you're double crossing me —" Finch began.

"I'll find him," said Carson.

Finch handed over Coburn's Colt revolver. "Don't kill him," he said, as Carson slipped down from the stone step and jogged around the side of the school. Still breathing hard, Finch pulled a flask from his vest pocket and took a long, hard pull.

"Bless you, Dorothy," Coburn whispered as, crouching in the school's root cellar, he reached for a short coach gun, covered in dust but no doubt functional. He'd feigned nostalgia for Carson's sake; far from sweet, Dorothy Kotraba had been a bigoted witch filled with old country conceit. She played favorites among the students, and Coburn was never teacher's pet.

The old buzzard wasn't afraid of much, but living close to the Ponca tribe gave her conniptions. The citizenry of Red Horizon thought the school's cellar was a storehouse for winter potatoes and a shelter from spring tornados, which it was, but it was also Miss Kotraba's last line of defense against the Indians. Being safe from floodwaters so high on the hill, it was well stocked with dry ammunition.

Emerging at the southwest corner of the school house, Bill Carson worked his way through a stand of trees and thistles, six-shooter in hand. Coburn stood twenty feet away next to a wood-capped hole in the ground, a cistern overgrown with nightshade and clover. Or maybe not a cistern?

"John," said Carson, lowering his gun. "Thank God I found you. Finch is around front."

"Tell me something . . . Bill."

"Okay, yeah, sure." Carson glanced to the left and right. "But make it quick."

"How'd you know my name? I never told you."

"Well, uh," Carson floundered, "I guess

Finch told me when he brought you into the cell."

Coburn nodded. "I thought maybe you recalled the time we spent together in Cheyenne."

"I don't follow you," said Carson.

"The real Marshal Bill Carson was in Cheyenne, at Tom Faraday's death bed. He knows exactly where the money is." Coburn stepped forward, and Dorothy Kotraba's short scattergun came up. "You see, I was standing there with him."

The imposter swung his arm up, but Coburn pulled the trigger, slamming buckshot into his chest, sending him backward into the woods.

Coburn crouched low and reloaded. At the sound of gunfire, would Finch come to investigate or high-tail it across the prairie? Greed brought him all the way to Red Horizon with a wagonload of dynamite. Finch wouldn't give up now.

Within minutes, Coburn knew he'd guessed right.

"I lied about your sister, Peregrine," said Finch from in front of the school. "She didn't die." Coburn gripped the shotgun and clenched his teeth together.

"She was too busy servicing the local gentry to die," said Finch.

Footsteps. Finch was walking forward, his steps deliberate and sure. "Come on out around here. I'll tell you more about the girl."

Another step.

"I'll tell you what she smelled like."

Another step.

"What she said in the heat of passion."

Another step.

Finch pivoted around the corner and fired off three quick shots.

There was no one there.

A short-barreled shotgun lay on the ground.

"Finch."

The big man spun, felt the impact, and saw the carved handle of Coburn's knife protruding from his chest. Without a fight, he fell to the ground and died.

Coburn let the buckskin drink from the trough outside the church. The scent of autumn was full in the air, but the earlier chill was past, and the day was warm and promised clear skies. It should be a good day for riding, and maybe, if he was lucky, a clue to the whereabouts of his family and his friends.

He turned, and his shadow crossed the fresh graves of Jacob Finch and his partner.

Back in Cheyenne, Faraday had confessed that he, Eli Sanders, and Jacob Finch had held up the stage before parting company to hide their loot. It was Sanders now lying in the ground next to Finch.

Before Faraday passed, he had told Coburn and Carson — the real Bill Carson — one thing more.

The Peregrine entered the church and walked to the base of the heavy walnut altar. He carefully pried off the top before reaching into the hollow space below for the canvas sack he knew would be there.

Borrowed Time

In the winter of '86, they pitched Kid Joseph straight into the warm yellow glow of the hotel lobby, not like a boy and not like a man, but trussed up like a shock of kindling to burn, the ropes around his wrists and ankles frayed and crusted with ice. Two bearded men on each side had hands on his elbows, and two more devils chuffed behind with shotguns and revolvers. They steered the Kid toward Kimbel at the front desk. From his post beside a straw-filled fainting couch, Daniel watched a reporter from *The River News* follow them in.

Kimbel jumped like a sack of cats and fumbled with the registration book. "Mister Moss," said Kimbel, filling in the ledger, "and Mister —"

"Captain," said Moss, full of frost. "Captain Edward Moss of Nebraska."

Daniel adjusted his cap and bit down on the small hunk of tobacco between his back teeth. When his mouth was full of the burned wood and apple taste of it, he swallowed, as he had learned to do since coming to work at the Grand Dakota Hotel.

"Of course, very good," stammered Kimbel as he scribbled. The shadows from the kerosene lamps danced across the patterned blue wall paper, and the hotelier looked quickly at Moss's hard face, then shivered with the wind. "Close the door, Daniel," said Kimbel, quiet but hard, like Daniel had left it open.

Kid Joseph, two years older than Daniel, whistled "Whiskey Parker."

"They wired us you'd be coming," said Kimbel, "but . . . well . . ." He fell silent as Moss introduced the other men, deliberately failing to mention the slender cargo shuffling his snow covered boots on the weathered oak floor.

"I really should have the prisoner's name," said Kimbel. "For the record, you understand."

Moss shook his head.

"Boy, take Captain Moss's bag," Kimbel hissed. Daniel did as he was told.

"Reckon we should find us something to eat," said Moss.

"Suits me, Cap'n," said the Kid, his lazy voice full of eighteen summers and invulnerable. "Why don't we rustle up a Christmas ham with all the trimmings?" He looked directly at Daniel then and gave him a wink, like he could slip away at any time.

One of the bearded men, Gardner, slapped the Kid's head, knocking his cap to the floor.

"No second helpings for you," said the Kid, and Daniel hid his smile with the effort of lifting Moss's satchel. He swallowed some chew again, and it left him feeling lightheaded.

"Please sir," Kimbel tried again. "The boy's name? Just for the record?"

The news reporter — Daniel thought his name was Barry — leaned forward with expectation, a pencil tapping softly at a small tablet.

Moss laughed, and Daniel let the bag slip to the floor. Baring yellow teeth, Moss pushed his charge forward. "This here is Arnold Joseph," he said, "heir to some of the greatest horse thieves in history." He paused like a preacher, his words hanging in the air.

A beat.

Two beats.

Not a preacher.

A showman.

"Slick as pig shit and twice as yellow," said Moss.

"That's the nicest thing you've said to me today," said the Kid, and all the men laughed.

The sole survivor of Bill Napier's gang and the bad goings in '83 and '84, Joseph allegedly earned his own chance for the gallows swiping a half dozen geldings from one of the big ranches in the Verdigris River Valley. The previous afternoon, word had come from Vermillion that Moss and his men had finally caught up with Joseph in an east Dakota cornfield. The road back to Nebraska led through Engle's Mill.

Daniel laughed too, then lugged the canvas bag over rugs and along the floor. Kimbel busied himself getting two heavy quilts from a cupboard in the wall, while Barry scratched out notes for the morning edition. The horseplay and wood heat had everyone more relaxed, but when Daniel locked eyes with Kid Joseph, he saw the older boy's gaze was rigid and dark.

Turning under Kimbel's scrutiny, Daniel led the party to a pair of adjoining rooms at the back of the building.

"You in the army, Captain?" said Daniel while carefully lighting the first room's lamp.

Moss pushed the Kid onto the feather mattress and untied his hands while Gardner kept the scattergun level. "You can call it that," he said. While Kimbel spread out the blankets, Barry stayed in the hallway, scribbling on his pad.

"We're an army of concerned men," said the man with the Colt.

"Ain't really none of your business, son," said Gardner.

"Give the boy something for his effort," said the Kid.

"I don't take orders from you," said Moss. Even so, he reached into his hip pocket.

"Not until the show," said the Kid. "Just wait until tomorrow."

"What show, Captain?" said Barry.

"Thought we might hold us a social event," said Moss. "Give everyone a chance to meet a bona-fide outlaw. Maybe you could arrange it?"

Moss pulled out a money clip, sterling silver and bent out of shape with a thick wad of bills. Daniel had never seen anything like it.

"What would you say to the fellowship hall of the Lutheran church?" asked Barry. "They're holding a basket dinner tomorrow."

"I'd say that suits us just fine."

"That coin's my property," said the Kid. "Any of you fellas keeping accounts?"

After handing the reporter a few bills, Moss peeled off five dollars and held it just beyond Daniel's grasp, "You fetch whatever we need, whenever we need it." Daniel eyed the money and nodded.

"For as long as we stay," added the big man.

The reporter could no longer keep his curiosity in check. "Is it true you caught the kid with his trousers down?"

"Was there gun play?" said Kimbel.

"When did you learn he was in Dakota?"

Moss held up a callused hand. When he spoke, his voice was heavy and flat as a smith's anvil, but the mirth of a circus ringmaster still danced in his eyes. "One at a time," he said. Moss had been on the Kid's trail for the better part of two years. Daniel could tell he was enjoying his time in the limelight.

"Why didn't you just find a good piece of hemp and a sturdy oak limb?"

"He'll be turned over to the proper authorities day after tomorrow," said Gardner before Moss could speak up. "Nice and proper."

"Ain't nobody here a killer," agreed Moss.

"Leastways, no convicted killers," said the

Kid, his eyes on Moss. "Whyn't you show everybody my watch?" he said.

Daniel hadn't seen Kimbel leave, but when his boss reappeared in the doorway, he carried a bottle of corn whiskey and glasses. While Kimbel handed out drinks, Moss reached into the pocket of his flannel coat and took out an ornate silver watch.

"This here is a key wind specimen of genuine silver," said Moss, raising the watch high into the candlelight, its hunter case returning a score of orange stars. Daniel had never seen a time piece so large or so beautiful. Like a living thing, it breathed in and out, and the liquid candle reflection slid around beveled curves and shone like the sun across the silver flat planes. "It's more than twice the size of regular pocket clocks. On a full year's wages, none of us here could buy such a treasure." Moss grinned, anticipating the punch line. "The Kid bought it outright with three day's earnings."

Eyes wide, Kimbel gasped with pleasure, and Barry shook his head. "Imagine such a thing," he whispered.

"I talked to the jeweler who sold it to him back east," added Gardner. "That thing's worth a fortune."

"More important," said Kid Joseph, "it

keeps good time."

"Time is all you got left," said Moss.

"So why don't you give some back to me?"

Moss chuckled, popped open the lid and pretended to peer into the glass. "I'd say you got about 72 hours."

"Let's have another drink anyway," said the Kid, and after Moss tucked the watch carefully away, everyone did, even Daniel.

Later, in his own room and drifting off to sleep, Daniel wondered about the Kid. What must it be like to be so free, to grow your hair long and not answer to anybody about anything. What would it be like to just live, to name things whatever you wanted to name them, to know you owned every rock and blade of grass, every rabbit and squirrel and every horse, whether someone had penned it up or not.

He had known freedom close to that only once, when he'd walked away from his family's eternal bickering and equally endless farm work to spend the night beside a whistling post, so that when awakened by the train, he might jump aboard and ride far away. But he didn't have Kid Joseph's courage; he couldn't yet lay claim to the wandering hills. He'd only ridden the train for a few miles, and a day later, he took the job at the hotel in Engle's Mill for room and board.

The next day, a gun in Kid Joseph's hand made two spinsters literally swoon and drop, so Moss reluctantly cut short that part of the show. "I assure you folks, there wasn't a bullet within reach."

Held at the ankles to a ring in the makeshift wood platform, Joseph shrugged, and Moss holstered the empty revolver.

"I hear he does a right fancy spin with that Colt," said someone.

"Heard he's a fast draw too."

At least a hundred people came and went and milled around the fellowship hall of the new Lutheran church. Through his smile, Moss quietly cursed himself. The men should've charged admission.

Kimbel stood close to the stove and a bubbling coffee pot, visiting with Barry as he handed out special editions of The River News. Those two had stayed up drinking together long after the rest of the hotel had gone to sleep. Thick as thieves.

"Let's have a hymn, Captain," called a tall man beside the player piano. With a nod, the old notes were pounded out.

Daniel leaned against a far back wall and read the newspaper.

Citizens of the northern plains are experiencing supreme relief at a requiem to months of terror. Unjustly menaced by a roughneck left over from inglorious days past, the people of our territory can thank their merciful Creator for the diligence of Captain Edward Moss and the good men of his company who valiantly tracked the heinous outlaw and horse thief Arnold Joseph into Dakota where the unchurched ruffian was found cowering in a corn field.

Around him, the crowd enjoyed the supreme relief Barry wrote about, but Daniel thought it owed less to the capture of Kid Joseph and more to the roaring wood stove and the tables filled with fruit breads, biscuits, and pie.

While expert gunplay on the part of Moss and Gardner was reportedly involved, it is the impression of the River News that eighteen-year-old Joseph ultimately had no stomach for a man's fight and surrendered readily to his betters. Quickly unarmed and thoroughly searched, Kid Joseph, as he's become known to some, was found to be in possession of not less than several hundred dollars, a heavy gold money clip, and a Swiss-made Chinese duplex watch of sterling silver.

"I heard the social presentation was the Captain's idea," said a man just under the din. "But obviously the Kid loves it."

"It's a good example for the children. Plenty of young men will think twice after today."

"Gives the people a chance to witness law and order first hand," said the first man.

"Moss ain't wearing a star," mumbled Daniel. "If you don't mind me saying so," he quickly added.

Both men stared blankly and moved away.

The time-piece is a rarity, its oversized hunter case dotted with glamorous Oriental detail; its bleached, stainless face showing a simple exquisite display. Arnold bragged to this paper that the piece keeps perfect time, but there too the boy comes up wanting. Due to an unfortunate defect in the clock's escapement, the otherwise smooth sweep of the second hand will jump now and again, eventually gaining a full minute for every passing ten.

When the song was done, Moss cleared his throat and again addressed the crowd.

"You farmers might work all year and still have barely enough to survive." He cocked his head at the Kid, who seemed to glow as he pulled the money clip with its thick packet from his shirt. "Yet this boy earned enough in a couple days for the clip alone."

The Kid bowed and grinned without a care in the world.

"And you ought to see his pocket watch! Of course it's stolen property, but we let him keep it." Daniel glanced around and saw that Moss owned the crowd, sending home the punch line with the voice of an accomplished showman. "Why not? He's living on borrowed time."

The laughter was deafening. When the Kid patted his flannel coat pocket, Daniel could tell that something was wrong. Moss turned, expecting to see the watch on display, but Joseph shook his head. Moss frowned and answered with a shrug.

Daniel realized Kimbel was beside him. "I need you to run over to the hotel," he said.

"What?" For a moment, Daniel couldn't think. Last night, Moss had slipped the watch into the pocket of his coat before he'd hung it in the room's tall wooden wardrobe. Daniel had seen him.

"Need you to get the big picnic basket," continued Kimbel. "Mr. Barry wants to put together a basket for his sister."

Daniel stared at his employer absently. "Mr. Barry."

"Yes, Mr. Barry's sister. The poor dear is bedridden," said Kimbel.

"Yes, sir," said Daniel, moving toward the door. He turned back, but Kimbel was already gone.

. . . the otherwise smooth sweep of the second hand will jump now and again . . .

Around him, everyone gasped with pleasure as Moss and the Kid spun twin lariats in a synchronous act. The tall man by the piano squealed with joy.

"You can always tell a horse thief by the way he swings a rope," he said.

Falling in with a boisterous family of Swedes, Daniel let himself be moved to the door, his thoughts trained on the hotel and all the hiding places there.

The church crowd had scarcely begun to break up when the north wind picked up, and the clouds again grew dark. The Captain's party agreed to spend the night in the home of Gardner's daughter and son-in-law across the Missouri, a short drive into Nebraska. With a few hours of daylight still ahead of them, they made ready to leave. One of the vigilance men brought the horses and wagon around to the front of the church, while Gardner and the others marched Kid Joseph out just as they'd brought him in. Tied at the wrists and ankles, he stood patiently under guard. Inside the church, Moss gave his farewells.

With a careful air of indifference, Daniel approached the wagon.

"Sir?" It was the first time he had spoken directly to the Kid.

"Son?" They were only two years apart, getting closer with each breath.

"I found your watch."

The Kid's eyes flickered and lit like a holiday candle. "So you did." Joseph watched as Daniel moved his hands across the cold silver casing. "Where was it?"

Kimbel and Barry tumbled from the church, talking loudly, laughing. When they saw Daniel holding the watch, they quickly looked away.

"It never left the hotel."

Joseph looked over his shoulder, but Kimbel and Barry were already shuffling down the street. His hands clasped, and so only Daniel could see, the kid made a gun from his thumbs and forefingers and pretended to fire at them.

As snow started to fall gently into the

street, the younger boy held out the time piece.

"No," said Joseph. "I'd like you to have it."

Captain Moss strode from the church, his scarf pulled around his face, his leather gloves looking stiff and ineffectual. He shouted at Gardner, "Get him the hell on board."

"C'mon Arnold."

"I understand it doesn't keep good time," said Daniel.

"Truly it don't," said the Kid, and Daniel nodded.

"Be well," said the Kid as he climbed up the wagon and sat next to Moss. "Full ahead, Captain," he said without looking back.

Daniel watched the wagon make two long tracks down the street and turn and vanish. He started to run ahead, maybe just to catch one more glimpse.

And then he stopped.

Be well.

"I will," whispered Daniel, and he turned and started to walk out of town, and just like that, the entire world opened up for him, and he knew he could have it.

"I'll be just fine."

No longer needing it, he pulled the hotel

cap from his head and launched it through the thickening snow.

He thought he knew where he could find a horse.

The Society of The Friends of Lester McGurk

The post office in Moosetrail, Wyoming, population 112, was a sturdy brick building with towering plate glass windows fronting a dusty boardwalk and street deep with ruts and rocky gutters. Inside, behind his polished counter and warmed by the sun rising in the eastern sky, new postmaster Augustus Crane breathed in deep, reveling in the business smell of the wide open room — leather bound ledgers, reams of cut paper, and perforated gummed stamps hinting vaguely of spearmint leaf.

He tore a sheet from his daily calendar and dust motes spun into the ether.

April 16, 1903.

His first day on the job.

Gus nudged a bottle of acrid India black ink on the counter to bring it in line with two other bottles, one red and one green.

He pushed a brass pen holder with its cedar stylus to the right.

Then an inch forward.

Then to the left.

With a twist of his bow tie, Gus turned to the row of windows and eyed his reflection with suspicion. His grimaced, gave his teeth a quick scrub with a finger, then patted his blonde head at the part where he'd combed out his curls with a healthy dollop of sweet bay rum tonic earlier that morning.

A young woman with a fringed blue parasol walked along the boardwalk.

Gus waved.

The woman passed by without so much as a nod.

He shrugged.

Getting to know folks took patience.

His position gave him a fine view of the Moosetrail Hotel and Snorty Horse saloon across the way. The buildings sat side by side, separated by only a narrow alley of red dust and weeds. Wood framed and sided with eggshell white planks, the three-story hotel with its blue canvas awning and wide entrance seemed protective of its one-room neighbor. There was a restaurant on the first floor and electric lights that came on at dusk. Men and women stood on the steps chatting after an early breakfast. Business men, ranchers, and a few sodbusters went in and out of the Stockman's Café as downtown came to life. The saloon had electricity too, but wouldn't open until after lunch. With its low-slung batwing doors and row of squat hitching rails, it was like a little brother, waiting his turn quietly in the shadows.

The morning wore on.

On his desk at the north wall was a copy of the Cheyenne newspaper, its headline announcing President Roosevelt's ongoing visit to Wyoming and several other western states. Gus had already read it twice.

He decided to pass some time by memorizing three yellow wanted posters tacked to the white plaster wall on his left. Deke Gruber. Ronald Clay. Malachi Smith. A confidence man, a bank robber, and a road agent. Either the sketch artist wasn't too very talented, or his subjects were some ugly dudes indeed.

Probably both.

On the opposite wall was a framed photograph of Gus from a few years ago. Second row, third from the left, he posed with Company B, jaunty in his cavalry uniform, a jungle in the background.

He checked his watch. The coach from Cheyenne, carrying the day's mail, was still an hour away.

He sighed, and again nudged the bottle of ink.

Above him, a tin ceiling fan clicked around and around, its electric motor slightly off-kilter.

When the brass bell over the door rang, Gus jumped to attention like a guilty schoolboy.

"Good morning, sir," he said, but the middle-aged customer dressed in denim and wearing a Stetson and spurs ignored him. The man was of African descent, and warm grey road dust clung to his jeans and vest.

He moved deliberately to the brass wall of locked postal boxes that filled the southern wall.

No pleasantries were apparently needed.

The compact mailboxes were numbered 1 to 60, and all of them — except for two — had names assigned to them.

The cowboy opened Box 13 with a key, placed something inside, then gently clicked the brass door closed, and turned to leave.

"I didn't catch your name, sir," said Gus.

"Lester McGurk," said the cowboy without stopping.

"Well, there's friendly and there's unfriendly," said Gus aloud as he watched the man quickly exit and stride across the street. "And that was decidedly unfriendly."

He shrugged again.

It was, after all, his first day on the job.

Gus pictured the gruff cowboy's face in his head and determined to do better next time he saw Mr. Lester McGurk.

For now, he'd collect the mail the man had errantly placed inside the box.

"Outgoing mail will be dropped in the appropriate dispensary or handed in at the counter," Gus recited to the empty room, "Incoming mail will be delivered to the appropriate box by the Postmaster. And only by the Postmaster"

But since the stage coach had yet to arrive, there was no incoming mail.

And yet, incoming mail was precisely what Gus found in Box 13.

Two crème colored envelopes addressed to the box with a flourishing hand, each sealed with a blob of bright, cherry colored wax.

Since the envelopes were properly addressed to the box with no return, Gus decided to leave them in place.

The cowboy must have made a mistake. Gus chose to overlook it this once.

But he wondered who Box 13 was registered to. Was it Lester McGurk's box? Or did it belong to somebody else? Why would a man deliver mail to himself?

"Let's find out," he said.

Gus pushed the current ledger aside, and from a shelf just under the counter pulled out an older, nearly identical book. A quick search found the records he wanted, and he ran his finger down the list of penciled names and adjoining box numbers.

The box was indeed registered to Lester D. McGurk, resident of Willow Siding, a whistle stop five miles down the mainline, southeast of Moosetrail.

Odd. Checking the ledger had offered no answers.

"Well, the next time Mr. McGurk comes in, I can greet him by name and at least inquire about his home town."

Gus looked up as the door bell announced a new customer.

The girl with the blue parasol.

She wasn't more than 24 or 25 years old, same as Gus, and when she pulled her umbrella shut, he was surprised to see her ring fingers were bare and even more shocked that her shimmering floor length sky-colored dress was slit up the side, revealing a glimpse of a tan laced garter around a long, lovely leg.

She had flashing green eyes and a blaze of red hair.

Swallowing, Gus hoped he wouldn't stutter.

"G-good morning."

Her smile was enough to send a tingle from the top of Tom's smooth combed mop to the tips of his toes.

Naturally, at just such a time, the door bell rang again.

This time the customer was a clean-shaven black-clad dandy sporting a string tie and wearing a hammer-claw suit coat. The gentleman entered the post office swinging a golf club with his left hand. The club had a wood shaft and a leather grip. The man looked for all the world as if he owned the place. Which, Gus thought, he most certainly did not because this whole building was the property of the United States government.

"May I help you?" asked Gus.

"I like a man with a bow tie," said the dude. His eyes were small and interesting in that the iris was abnormally dark, blending with the pupil to coal black. "Your hair's a bit long though, son. You might want to see Doc Tanner for a trim."

Gus brushed at the back of his neck.

"Can I get you some stamps, or . . . ?"

"No thank you," said the man. "I can manage."

Then he walked straight to Box 13.

Producing a key from his pocket, he reached out and turned the lock. After removing an envelope from inside, he closed the box.

Gus pursed his lips. "What goes on?" he said. This popinjay certainly wasn't the cowboy Lester McGurk.

Gus addressed the man as he moved to leave the office.

"Excuse me? Do you have business with Mr. McGurk?"

Holding the envelope to his chest, the man arched his brows. "Excuse me?" he said.

"I wondered if Mr. McGurk knew that you were collecting his mail."

"I'm Lester McGurk," said the man.

Then he turned on his heel and with a swing of his golf club walked quickly from the office, whistling as he left.

"Are you all right, sir?" said the woman with the blue parasol. "You've gone quite red in the face."

"That man said his name was McGurk."

"Well, naturally," she said, "that's because it was Mr. McGurk."

"I see," said Gus.

He watched then as — gliding across the polished hardwood floor without a sound, the woman went directly to Box 13. She opened the box with a key, removed the second envelope waiting there, and shut the door with a gentle click.

Parasol in hand, the woman turned to leave, envelope tucked away in a place Tom tried not to think about.

"Hold on," said Gus.

"Yes?"

"It's some sort of joke, is it?"

"What?"

"This Box 13 business. There seems to be something highly improper — if not unlawful — going on, Miss." Gus put some authority into his voice. "Miss?"

"McGurk," said the woman.

Then, with a quick smile she was gone.

For five minutes, Gus stood alone in the empty post office, staring out at the empty street and the opposite row of buildings, wondering about Box 13 and the trio of individuals claiming the name McGurk.

Somebody — more than one somebody — seemed to be having great fun at his expense.

That's when the blue parasol caught his eye coming down the steps of the hotel. Incredibly, the redhead crossed the boardwalk and moved directly to the batwing doors of the Snorty Horse saloon. In her hand, she held a slim crème colored square.

Gus was sure it was the envelope from Box 13. It had to be! Especially since she'd just pulled it out of — out of — well, there!

And then, even more incredibly, one of the men from the Wanted posters stepped out on the boardwalk.

Gus knew the road-agent immediately from his picture, a pock-marked ox whose blonde bristled chin ran down into his shiftless neck like milky white crick water.

Exactly like his poster.

The artist wasn't too bad after all. The likeness was dead on.

Malachi Smith nodded and took the letter from the redhead's outstretched hand.

When the stage coach came in with two bags of mail from Cheyenne, Gus put the Box 13 affair out of his mind — relieved to perform his assigned duties at last.

But he didn't sleep well that night, so he was thankful the next day was a short one.

The stage coach ran only twice a week. On off days, the post office opened for a few hours in the morning — just long enough for folks to post a letter or pick up something they'd missed the day before — before closing precisely at 12 noon.

Gazing across at the Snorty Horse saloon from his place behind the counter that second morning, Gus again saw Malachi Smith with the redhead. This time she was dressed in a long scarlet affair with matching parasol.

A known outlaw consorting with Miss McGurk. In broad daylight. And Gus was sure it had something to do with the crème colored envelopes.

Sworn to uphold the sanctity of the United States mail after his time in the service during the Spanish war, Gus tasted iron. He chewed his lip, and in spite of the cool spring weather and the clicking fan overhead, his back began to sweat.

He looked at the photograph of his old cavalry unit. Gus hadn't seen the worst of things in the Spanish war, but he'd seen enough. He knew when something nefarious was happening right under his nose.

Back in Cheyenne at the office where he'd first cut his teeth, he would've made out a typed report for his supervisor.

Now there was nobody to report to but himself.

No typewriter either. (He made a note to see about getting one.)

But the authorities of law and order would need to be notified.

As if on cue, the door bell rang, and the dandy-in-black version of Lester McGurk walked in, golf club casually in hand. The man tipped his Vaquero-style hat back with a forefinger.

"You were wondering about the law?

"I was?" Gus stammered. "But . . . how, I mean that is . . . when . . . ?"

"You mentioned unlawful activities last night to Miss McGurk. I wanted to follow up."

Gus narrowed his eyes.

"It's alright, son. I'm a United States marshal," said the man.

"Marshal McGurk?"

"Something like that," the man smiled. "What is it you wanted to talk about?"

"The . . . ah, young lady," said Gus. "With the parasol. She told me her name was also McGurk."

"Family," said the marshal.

"And the cowboy who also goes by that name?" Gus straightened up tall and put both hands firmly on the counter. "Don't tell me he's part of your family?"

The marshal cocked his head and grinned. "He is."

"And he has a key to Box 13?"

"He does."

"How many other members of your family also have keys, sir?"

"I expect there are an even dozen keys

amongst the friends of Lester McGurk."

"As I declared to Miss McGurk last night, it's highly irregular. There are only two keys issued per post office box."

"I see." The marshal held his golf club perpendicular to floor, eyeing an imaginary ball. "Was there anything else?" he said.

"How about the flagrant presence of a known outlaw?" Gus nodded toward the notice on the wall. "I saw Malachi Smith just this morning."

"Of course you did." The marshal's attention still at the floor. Then: "Do you play golf, Mr. Crane?"

"Do I what?" said Gus.

"Play golf?"

"I do not play golf."

"Cards?"

"On occasion."

"Poker, by chance?"

"On occasion."

"Delightful!" snapped the marshal. "Just delightful. I'm sure we'll get along fine." He tucked the club under his arm and turned to go. "Be sure to check the Box before you lock up today," he said.

"Box?"

But the marshal was already out the door.

Of course he'd been referring to Box 13.

Inside, Gus found another crème colored

envelope.

An envelope he never posted.

Nor had it been there the night before when — as part of his duties — he had checked each box before closing.

And nobody had been in the office that morning except him and the marshal.

But here was the envelope, just the same.

And this time the name in the stylish address was his:

Augustus Crane
Box 13
Moosetrail, Wyoming

Gus broke the wax seal.

Tonight on Hempstreet Road.
The cabin at Millbrook.
Come alone.

The invitation was signed in the ornamental hand of Lester McGurk.

During the war, Gus became an accomplished horseman.

Through both instinct and necessity, he shared a rapport with his mount that many of his comrades envied. When it came to Gus Crane, the steeds never knew a stranger. The young soldier, now the duly appointed Postmaster of Moosetrail, had them literally eating out of his hand.

On Hempstreet Road they paralleled the railroad tracks for more than a mile. When the yelps of distant coyotes cut loose and his roan gelding shuddered, Gus was one step ahead.

"Shhh, fella," he said, petting the withers, scratching at the ears, soothing the animal's trepidation with his tone of voice and actions.

In the distance, Gus heard the mournful low of a train whistle moving away from them. He couldn't help but wonder what kind of passengers would be traveling across the high plains so late at night.

The horse walked on, even as the yips continued rolling over the hills and into the scrub-filled canyon they entered. The air smelled of sage and ragweed and the echoing barks made it seem there were coyotes on all sides. Gus spoke reassuringly to his mount. "You have nothing to worry about," he said. "They're tricksters. Ventriloquists. I guarantee you, there aren't more than two or three at most. It's all a deception."

Which made him think again of the McGurks.

An even dozen keys, the marshal had said.

If he was a marshal.

Gus hadn't seen a badge.

Anybody could claim to be a marshal.

And anybody might lure an unsuspecting Postmaster into a trap.

That thought had brought August Crane and his nervous horse to Hempstreet Road well prepared and well armed.

In case the coyotes got too close, a lever-action Winchester rode in the saddle boot.

And — under his long dark coat, in a shoulder rig of his own design — Gus carried a 1902 Colt semi-automatic pistol acquired in the Sandhills just before moving to Wyoming.

In case the McGurks got too close.

They rode down a short incline toward a curve in the road. Above the blue-black cedar tree line, Gus made out a column of wispy smoke in the moonlight.

Millbrook Road was less than a half mile ahead.

His pulse began to race, but he squeezed the reins and reminded himself to breathe as they'd taught him in the cavalry, keeping his wits keenly on edge but not so sharp as to do more damage than good.

Casually, he rode around the bend and stopped back a ways, about twenty feet shy of the long, low-backed cabin.

The place had a flat roof eight or nine feet off the ground in front. Then it sloped back to a wall not more than five feet high.

Like a big chicken coop.

A window with four cloudy glass panes showed a soft lantern burning inside — coal oil, not electric.

And yet, curiously, a series of tall poles with round insulators and telegraph wire strung between them led from a rear corner of the cabin away across a short prairie and into the twisting canyon beyond.

As soon as he dismounted, the cabin door opened.

The African cowboy McGurk greeted him. "Hello, Crane. Glad you could join us."

Gus nodded. "I expected you might be here."

"We're all here," he said. "Let me take your horse out back with the others."

"I'd prefer to do it," said Gus.

"Suit yourself," said the cowboy.

In the grass behind the house, under the telegraph wires, Gus found a buckskin gelding, a paint, and another roan picketed some thirty feet apart. A high-wheeled wagon was parked next to a short haystack that was out of the animals' reach. Gus tied his horse to one of the poles between the wagon and the hay, pulled the rifle from his saddle, and walked back to the front of the house.

He knocked on the door.

The cowboy allowed him in to the cramped room with its sooty smell and few furnishings. As his eyes adjusted to the light, Gus recognized the two figures seated at a central oak table.

The marshal McGurk sat on the left. The redhead, now dressed in a forest green dress, sat on the right, her matching emerald parasol closed and leaning in the corner. Two chairs on the side opposite the cabin's door were pulled back and vacant. When the cowboy pulled the door shut it felt like they were closed inside a kitchen cupboard.

"You won't need that shooting iron," said the marshal, waving at Gus's rifle. "Or the one under your coat."

"I guess I'll be the judge of that," said Gus.

"Oh let him keep them," said the woman, ignoring the marshal.

The place was primitive, more of a storage shed than living space. Furnished with a table, six chairs, a cookstove, and a safe, each fixture was literally an arm's reach from the other. There was nothing in the way of additional hardware, and only one framed picture hung on the wall beside the door.

Strangely, the picture was covered with a black curtain.

The marshal McGurk stood up and opened the safe. "Sit down, Mister Crane," he said.

Just as Gus stooped to pull over a seat, the front door opened behind him.

He whirled around, rifle in hand and came face to face with Malachi Smith.

"Howdy there, pard," said the outlaw with a wide open smile. Then he looked past Gus toward the others. "Got that gol-damned wire repaired again, boss. Telegraph should work again."

Telegraph?

Gus remembered the poles outside and glanced to a far corner of the room where a short table held a sending-receiving unit under a row of dry-cell batteries.

"Who are you people?"

"Jumpy one, ain't he?" said Smith.

Gus spun back around, still gripping the rifle.

"You're a wanted man," he said flatly.

"Oh, pooh," said the redhead. "He's just the opposite."

"Outlaw just for the duration," laughed Smith, brushing past Gus and letting his ample weight crash down onto a chair. "C'mon mailman," he said pointing at the tall stool. "Sit down a spell."

"Smith is a lawman," said the marshal. "We all are." He smiled at the redhead. "Law people."

From the safe, the marshal removed an envelope.

"Welcome, Mister Crane," he said.

"You can . . . call me Gus."

"All right. Gus."

The cowboy sat down next to Smith, and the four of them faced him looking for all the world like a wide-eyed church choir.

Still standing, Gus again asked, "Who are you people?"

"I told you before," said the marshal. "United States Marshal. My name is Reece Landry."

"Police constable," said Malachi Smith. "From Dearborn, Michigan."

"United States Secret Service," said the redhead. "Call me Bess O'Connor."

"And I'm with the parks department over at Yellowstone," said the cowboy. "Bill Ellison."

"But you call yourselves McGurk? I don't understand."

"Your predecessor was our postmaster and Sheriff of the county," said Landry. "I've arranged for you to be appointed Sheriff. Next time Justice Taylor's in town, that is."

"I don't understand."

Landry held out the envelope. "Read this."

It was identical to the others Gus had seen at the post office. Creme colored, sealed with red wax.

Gus pulled the envelope from Landry's grip, hurriedly tore it open, then pulled out the handwritten note inside.

He started to read the same hand writing that was used on the other Box 13 envelopes.

"This can't be real," he muttered.

When finished, he read the note again. Then a third time. Finally, he laid it on the table.

"That's not exactly a friendly letter," he said.

"Consider it an invitation," said Landry.

"More of a draft notice," said Gus.

"The Society of the Friends of Lester McGurk," said Landry.

"With my assigned duties coming from Box 13," said Gus.

"Just like the rest of us."

"The note mentions danger."

"In the performance of certain duties," said Landry. "In the pursuit of law and order."

"Naturally," said Smith.

"And this place?" said Gus.

"Railroad property," said Ellison.

Gus recalled the train's receding tones.

"Bill mans the telegraph. We meet here only when absolutely necessary," said Landry.

"Are there others?"

"Assuredly," said Bess.

"What's it gonna be, Gus?" said Smith.

"I've never belonged to a secret society before," said Gus.

"Join us," said Bess. "You'll be on the side of justice. You'll be on the side of right. And you can always count on us, as we'll count on you."

"How can I say no?"

"You can't," said Landry. "To us you could, but not to him."

Gus picked up his invitation from the table even as the marshal pulled the dark curtain away from the presidential portrait on the wall.

At the bottom of the note, signed by one T. Roosevelt, in parentheses it said, "aka: Lester D. McGurk."

Gus smiled and tossed the note to the table. "You'll excuse me if I suggest all of you have lost your minds." Gripping his rifle, he walked to the door, "I'll just wish you a good night."

He jerked open the door.

"And a beautiful night it is," said the stocky man standing there, cigar in hand. "Just listen to those coyotes."

Gus stepped back and blinked quickly.

Surely not.

The bespectacled man laughed. "I've had a long train ride, son. Aren't you going to invite me in?"

Surely.

"Of course," said Gus. "Of course, Mr. President."

April 26, 1903

"I still can't believe he'd travel all that way just for our meeting," said Gus with the same breathless tone he'd been using with Bess for the past week. "I mean, all the way to Moosetrail from Yellowstone."

"Moosetrail isn't so terribly far from Mr. McGurk's current entourage in Yellowstone. Certainly not as far as his home in Washington. And certainly not by private rail," said Bess. "He was here and back again before anybody could notice."

They were strolling along the boardwalk, arm in arm, heedless of the townspeople who stared after them. Bess O'Connor had been in Moosetrail for a month posing as the widow of an eastern cattleman, checking on her estate. As such, she'd never been without a companion or invitation to dinner. Now that it appeared the lucky young Postmaster was well on his way to becoming a cattle baron, tongues couldn't stop wagging.

"You're not having doubts are you?" she said. "About joining us?"

"It's a lot to take in."

"We need to know we can count on you. John Bartlett could already be in town."

"You're convinced the intelligence you've gathered about him is reliable?"

"I have no doubt. All along the eastern seaboard John Bartlett is a known demolitions expert, as well as being a confirmed anarchist. If Mr. McGurk believes Bartlett will be causing trouble during his whistle stop tour of the West, we have to take the threat seriously."

Gus nodded and held Bess's hand as she stepped off the boardwalk.

"Since President McKinley was killed, our mission has expanded. My friends take all threats very seriously."

"Threats?" said a voice, and they turned to see a slim man with a dark mustache and derby hat join them in the street.

"I couldn't help but overhear," the man

said, and Bess shot Gus a dirty look. "Is this man troubling you."

"Why, no," said Bess with a bright smile. "Not at all, Mr. Norbert. Not at all."

"Norbert?" said Gus.

"Just watching out for the lady's welfare, sonny."

"Mr. Crane is our postmaster," said Bess. "This man is Mr. Norbert," said Bess. "He is a drummer who deals in scented bath salts and assorted soap. He's offered me the opportunity to share supper with him on two separate occasions."

"And I don't take kindly to anybody threatening Mrs. O'Connor in any way."

"I've had to decline both times," Bess explained.

"I should expect so," said Gus. He kept his eyes level, locked on Norbert's gaze.

Norbert put his hand on the postmaster's shoulder. "Let's talk about it man to man."

"Let's not."

Gus brushed away the hand.

"I'm not afraid of you," said Norbert. "I've got three inches and ten pounds on you. And at least ten years more experience." He scowled down at Gus. "What do you have?"

The postmaster smiled. "I've got the law on my side, Mr. Gruber."

"Gruber? How did you know — ?"

The instant Deke Gruber was distracted, Bess stepped back and swung her closed parasol around to smash into his jaw. Knocked sideways, Gruber stumbled into a nearby hitching post with a thud.

As the wanted man regained his balance, Gus stepped forward allowing his coat to fall open and reveal the new Sheriff's star there, as well as the Colt and shoulder rig.

"He's got a knife, Gus," said Bess.

"I got a knife," Gruber smirked like a kid on Christmas morning. "I don't know how you knew me, but it won't do you no good now."

"You don't know how I knew you?" said Gus. "I'm the postmaster! Your ugly pan is the first thing I see every morning."

Gruber stood with his legs wide apart, like he was riding an invisible two foot tall horse, he put his arms out like a circus acrobat. In one hand was a folding pocket knife, its short blade reflecting the morning sun.

He looked from Gus to Bess, then back at Gus.

"This was a set up, wasn't it?"

Gus didn't hesitate.

He stepped forward and, hard as he could, landed the toe of his boot between Gruber's legs.

The wanted man rolled to the ground, grabbing at his guts like a rodeo clown.

"Now it's your turn not to move," said Gus, scooping the knife up from the street.

The villain stayed on the ground, a curled up mass.

"Are you alright, ma'am?" said Gus as a few cowboys lingered on the boardwalk to watch.

"Naturally," said Bess.

"Deke Gruber," said Gus. "Wanted in three states for armed robbery and general brutality."

"Doesn't seem especially brutal, does he?" Bess said, giving him a small poke with her shoe.

Rocking back and forth, Gruber groaned. Tried to sit up, failed miserably and fell backwards.

Gus took a step forward anyway. "Stay down, you," he said.

"You handled yourself well," said Bess. "Your army service is showing."

"Not so much army as growing up with three brothers. Working for my dad, out in the middle of nowhere, there wasn't that much to do." He smiled at the memory. "Ride horse, hunt a stray cow. Get punched by your brother."

"Punch him back."

"Yeah."

Her eyes twinkled and the tingle went through Gus again as it always did, top to bottom.

Even as Gus felt his face flush in response to Bess's smile, Gruber took advantage of their conversation to find his feet and limp away down the street.

They watched as he ambled north, past the corner of the Snorty Horse and toward a patchy grass range.

"You know, he's not much of a runner, either," said Bess. "I wonder how he's eluded the law for so long?"

Gus drew the gun and bent to give Bess a peck on the cheek. "Be right back," he said.

That evening, after Gruber was securely behind bars, they continued their conversation at the hotel.

Before the meal, they sipped coffee and watched shadows grow under the Café's wide blue boardwalk awning.

"Listen to this," said Gus, rattling the pages of that day's edition of the Wyoming Tribune. "The good citizen back of the law counts most." He laid the paper aside and picked up his coffee cup. "A direct quote from the President today — delivered from the back of his 70-foot long railroad car in Newcastle, Wyoming."

He peeked around the edge of the paper.

The Stockman's Café took up the entire first floor of the hotel with room for twelve four place tables and a long narrow serving board down the east side. The square oak tables were covered with blue checked cloth that complimented walls of white plaster trimmed in heavy blue paint. Some of the plates were fine china, some were tin. The cutlery would never be mistaken for silver. Yet there was value in the place, a sense of cleanliness and care for the way food should be prepared. The air was just starting to fill with the smell of warm vegetables and stewed beef.

Bess's reply was candid, and Gus was grateful that this early in the evening the place was mostly deserted.

"Us good citizens better stop wasting time on small fry like Gruber and concentrate on the larger task at hand," said Bess.

Her tone was impatient. Her face more serious than he'd seen it.

"Somebody had to put Gruber behind bars," said Gus with a reassuring smile. "You don't regret helping out?"

Bess was adamant. "I need to see John Bartlett in jail next to him. I need to see Mr. McGurk safe at his home back east."

Her eyes shone brightly in the electric

light, and her perfume lingered on his suit-coat.

"And then?"

"Then I'll share my list of regrets."

Gus hadn't seen this side of her before. Sipping his coffee, he chose his next words with care.

"I wonder how Smith is doing with the Bar-7 men. The mail will be in from Cheyenne tomorrow. Maybe we'll hear something."

"And Bill will be at the cabin in the evening," said Bess. "The Marshal is due to check in as well."

Gus finished his coffee, recalling the details Lester McGurk laid out at their cabin meeting.

John Bartlett usually worked alone, but Reece Landry knew the bomber had ties with a group of anarchist sympathizers in Wyoming. A few of these men were known to receive lodging and financial support from the Bar-7 ranch outside Moosetrail. If Bartlett was planning to lash out at the President during his whistle-stop tour of the West — and he was, according to reputable sources in both the Pinkerton agency and the President's old Dakota ranch connections — then he'd likely make contact with the Bar-7. When he did, he'd run into a fellow outlaw named Malachi Smith who had recently found employment there. Smith would befriend Bartlett and lead him to Reece Landry, who would take both of them into custody.

Meanwhile, Gus and Bess were to monitor the hotel in Moosetrail and act as backup while Bill Emerson maintained telegraph communications with the President's party.

Meanwhile had lasted for more than six days with no word from Malachi Smith.

They'd all been given a description of Bartlett, along with a recent photograph. The hooligan was tall with shoulder length dark hair and a dark, brushy beard.

So far, nobody in Moosetrail had fit that description.

Gus understood his partner's impatience, and when he found himself chewing his lip again the next morning at the post office, he had second thoughts about the entire affair.

"Lawdy me, I don't believe you've heard a single word," said Minnie Drury, tapping an open page of the counter ledger with rough chewed fingernails. "Aren't you feeling well, Mr. Crane?"

The scolding tones cut through his meanderings and Gus straightened his shoulders.

"I'm sorry Miss Minnie," he said. "It's the heat, you know. Hardly spring time and it's already like summer. I don't catch a wink of sleep most nights." Gus shook his head and pushed a loose curl of hair back from his forehead. "You were saying?"

"Can't sleep you say?" Minnie's cackle was like eggs frying in a cast iron skillet. "When I was your age I could pass out just about anywhere, no matter the heat, cold or the good Lawd's apocalypse."

As she droned on, Gus's eyes moved over the street and across the front of the Snorty Horse and the Hotel. Nothing there, as usual.

Again, he started chewing his lip.

The mail from Cheyenne had been sparse, and once again there was nothing for Box 13.

No word from Malachi Smith.

Across the street, he caught a glimpse of red hair and saw Bess walk in to the hotel with Reece Landry.

"Can I get you some stamps today, or . . . ?" said Gus.

"Stamps? Oh, no." Minnie brushed off the request and it's implications. Instead, she plowed head long into her third long-winded story of the morning. "Had I told you about my sister's boy, Mr. Crane? Now there is a sad case."

"I believe I have some other customers," said Gus when a short man appeared on the boardwalk.

Minnie let her next sentence fade as the door opened and bell chimed. The fellow's wine-colored corduroy coat was worn smooth. His waxed blonde mustache was nearly as slick. "Good morning," he said.

"Yes it is," agreed Gus. "What can I do for you?"

"I'd like a dozen stamps, please."

"Yes, indeed," said Gus, happy for the interruption in Minnie's never-ending tirade.

"Would you happen to have any 1901 4-cent automobiles?"

Gus nodded as he pulled a tray of stamps from under the counter. "Are you a collector, sir?"

"The short man plucked at his bushy blonde mustache. "Assuredly."

Gus counted out twelve of the commemorative stamps with their colorful borders and black center image of a B&O railroad electric car. "Red or brown?"

"Six of each?"

Gus handed them over. The short man paid with a gold dollar.

"The automobile stamps are always a

favorite," said Gus. "I don't have a lot of them left."

"I don't wonder. They're quite magnificent."

"What's this you're talking about," said Minnie, poking her nose back over the counter.

The man slid one of the stamps toward her. "The 1901 Pan-American issue," he said. As if everybody knew what he was talking about.

"Oh, just some old stamp?"

"There's more than one," said Gus.

"There are six distinct stamps, Madame," said the short man. "Issued in Buffalo, New York at the advent of the 1901 World's Fair." He smiled and turned back to Gus. "One of our nation's most auspicious events, wouldn't you agree?"

Gus smiled politely. "I wasn't there," he said.

The man's response was sympathetic. "Oh, I was," he said with enthusiasm. "I was, indeed. And auspicious is hardly enough of a word for the occasion."

"Exciting?" said Gus.

"High-falootin'?" said Minnie.

"Life changing!" said the man. Carefully he placed the stamps inside a long calfskin wallet and, secured inside his old jacket, turned to leave. "I thank you," said the man.

"Come back any time, Mister . . . ?"

"Butler," said the man. "Augustus Butler."

"Fancy that, sir. Augustus is my name, too."

"Are you new in town, Mr. Butler?" said Minnie.

"Just passing through," said Butler. "I'm into dry goods. First time on my new route." He paused, then added, "First time west of the Mississippi."

As Gus watched Butler leave, another customer entered. This was Agnes Tooms, Miss Minnie's cousin from Colorado.

"There she is," Agnes announced, rattling the windows. "I've been all over town looking for you."

"Lawd, is it that near noon time?" Minnie shook her head. "Mr. Crane and I have been visiting."

"Can't blame you for that," said Agnes, joining them at the counter. "Best looking man in town."

"You say that about all the men, Aggy."

"Oh, you!"

"Well, you do!"

"How are you then, Mr. Crane?"

"Mr. Crane?"

But right then Gus wasn't paying any attention to the chatty spinsters. Right then his attention was riveted on the tall man who reigned in a steeldust gelding at the hotel hitching rail. A tall man with long, dark hair and a bushy beard who left his steed stand untethered in the street while he mounted the boardwalk under the blue awning.

Gus watched John Bartlett enter the hotel and wondered if Bess and Reese Landry were also watching.

The Society of the Friends of Lester McGurk met that night in the rear of the post office next to a cot where Gus Crane had been spending his nights. "Just until I find a room," he explained. The room was lit with a single electric bulb and if Bess noticed his red face as he balled up some stray laundry, she didn't let on.

"Thank you all for coming here on such short notice," said Landry. "I didn't want to risk meeting at the cabin and losing track of Bartlett." He walked to the counter, then around and to the front of the open room where he gazed through the window at the steeldust horse still hitched at the rail across the street.

Gus slid a small table out into the middle of the room behind the counter. "I think we're ready," he said.

Normally a cheerful, tidy place of business, the nighttime room was full of eerie half shadows cast by the inside bulb and a waxing bright moon. During his time in Moosetrail, the place had literally become home to Gus. Now the click of the fan filled him with trepidation, and the sickly sweet spearmint gum of the stamps turned his stomach.

Best to get this done as quick as we can, he thought.

Gus, Bess, and Bill Ellison pulled up folding wooden chairs and sat down.

They met without Malachi Smith — who was still missing.

They listened to the marshal's report.

"A nice operator, this John Bartlett. Ever the polite cowboy, he's got everybody at the hotel under the spell of his charms."

"What name is he traveling under?" said Bess.

"His own, if you can believe this man's brass." Landry's palms faced upwards. "But why not? Who would recognize the name way out here? He certainly isn't expecting anybody to be on to his plot."

"And what about Smith?" said Gus.

"What about Smith? There's been nothing in the mail."

Gus shook his head.

"Nothing over the wires."

Bill Ellison had to agree.

"Malachi Smith's fate is a mystery."

Bess leaned forward and Gus again saw raw impatience. "You're a Federal Marshall, Reese. Why not snatch Bartlett up? Question him?"

"Make the devil tell us what happened to Smith," agreed Gus.

"Oh yes, absolutely," said Landry. "Threaten him, maybe? Beat him? Torture him?" The marshal stood up and leveled his finger at each of them in turn. "We do that and we may never see Smith again. Nor do we learn anything more about this so-called plot."

"What do we know about the plot?" said Bess. "That Bartlett wants to end the life of a man we've all sworn to protect? That he intends to do it sometime, somewhere — anywhere." She spread her arms wide.

"She's right, Marshal," said Gus. "We know damned little."

"Where do we start getting answers if not with Bartlett?" said Bess.

"And what about Smith?"

"Smith knew the risks." said Bess. "We can't let his welfare concern us. Not when we have the man we want right here and right now."

"Do we?" said Bill.

"Do we what?"

"Do we have him right here and right now?"

"His horse is still there," said Landry. "And when I left, the Stockman's Cafe had him stuffed with dinner and half asleep with ten year old whiskey."

"But for how long?" said Bill.

"We can't let him slip from our fingers," said Bess. "Like it or not, Smith is expendable."

Landry nodded and pushed out his lower lip. "I can't say I agree. But then, I can't disagree, either? What do you think, Crane?"

Gus weighed the question in his mind. Leaving Bartlett free to harm the President was out of the question. And they had no real proof that Smith had ever made contact with the man.

Truth be told, Smith might still be waiting for Bartlett at the Bar-7. Or he might have suffered an accident while there, and none of them would be the wiser.

"I say we snatch Bartlett up. Now. Tonight." Gus nodded toward a ring of keys hanging on a peg beside the office back door. "We can keep him in the city jail, if you'd like."

"I like," said Bess, flashing him a smile. "I

keep forgetting you're the sheriff of Moosetrail."

Landry nodded. "Alright, then. All in favor of capturing John Bartlett and holding him in the jail until we sort things out?"

The vote was unanimous.

As one, the four of them stood and folded their chairs together. Gus slid the table back into a corner and leaned the chairs beside it.

He took the iron ring of keys from the peg and stuffed them into his pocket. Just when he reached for the light switch, a heavy pounding came at the back door.

Each of the friends stood still while the pounding came again.

Landry whispered, "Who?"

"Somebody wanting their mail?" said Bess.

"Bartlett?" said Bill.

A voice from outside. "Let me in you polecats! I know you're in there."

"Not Bartlett," said Gus.

"Gol-dammit, open this cussed door."

"Smith!" said Bess, jumping forward to fling open the door.

Gus stood back and let the big man enter.

"About durned time," said Smith. "I've been looking for you folks all over town and I finally find you here."

Gus smiled. He couldn't help but think about Miss Minnie and her cousin, Agnes.

"It seems to be going around today," he said.

"What does?"

"Never mind," said Gus, slapping Smith on the back. "Never mind. Just tell us where you've been."

"And what you know about Bartlett?"

"Where I've been is following that sonuvabuck all over the country. What I know is damn little. We hooked up at the Bar-7 like I hoped. I rode with him a while, shared coffee at line camp yesterday morning. Then he gave me the slip in a canyon northwest of Laramie. I don't know where he's got to, but I figured I might as well get back here and see what you all knew."

"Don't you know? Bartlett is here," said Bess.

"Here in Moosetrail?" said Smith.

"Rode in late this afternoon," said Landry. "He's over at the hotel."

"We were just about to . . . ah, pay an official call on him," said Gus.

"Hell's bells!" said Smith. "If that don't tickle my whiskers. Here I follow him all the way from the Bar-7 all the way to Crow Creek and 'round these stinkin' pear shaped rocks at McGee's ranch and he ends up here in Moosetrail." Smith shrugged. "Makes me wonder why I bothered."

"Makes me wonder what he's up to," said Landry. "Let's go find out."

But it wasn't to be, because just as he said it, a bright flash illuminated the inside of the post office, the air was full of thunder, and the second and third story of the hotel across the street erupted in a magnificent orange and black ball of fire that hurtled chunks of wood and white planking high into the sky.

May 30, 1903

Gus Crane stood in front of a red, white and blue decorated wooden stage with Bess and Landry Reece waiting for their chance to shake hands with the President. A crowd of more than 3,000 had turned out that sun-drenched morning in Laramie to gather at the University amphitheater and hear Roosevelt reaffirm his commitment to the average man, honor war veterans and generally build up esteem for western America. Now that the speech was over, a highly publicized 65-mile horseback ride from Laramie would substitute for the President's train, conveying him and his party of 11 high-ranking dignitaries to the Capitol in Cheyenne. It was just the sort of stunt folks loved, thought Gus — and people like him dreaded.

As he watched the row of University officials file past Roosevelt, followed by city, county and state leaders, all with outstretched arms, ready hands and broad smiles, he reflected on his new perspective. Any one of those well-wishers — the average citizenship the President had so glowingly referenced — any one of them could hold a knife, gun, or bomb. Any one of them might be another Leon Czolgosz — the anarchist steel worker who killed President McKinley — somebody who could bring disaster in an instant.

But they weren't present today to protect Roosevelt. Others were doing that job, as Bess had assured them after checking in with her fellows in the Service.

They were there to celebrate the final leg of their benefactor's western tour.

And maybe, Gus hoped, a pat on the back for a job well done.

Landry stepped aside and allowed him to move ahead in line. Gus answered the marshal's smile with one of his own and reached for Bess's hand. He gave it a gentle squeeze and they both stepped forward.

As for their own would-be assassin, he had been killed in the Moosetrail Hotel fire of his own making. John Bartlett's body — or what was left of it — was found and identified in the wreckage. There was no doubt about it. A sad situation for the good people of Moosetrail, who lost a dozen good folks, but a fitting end to a horrendous plot. It could have been so much worse.

If he could, Gus would give each of the twelve dead citizens a medal commemorating their service to their country.

But there were no medals among the society of the Friends of Lester McGurk.

The President climbed four stairs back up to the podium.

Apparently there were no handshakes either.

As the crowd clapped and cheered, several other men mounted the steps and Gus watched as a score of folks to the right gave way for three men leading a trio of horses. More horses and more men followed.

"That's Yellowbird," said Bess. "That's the horse donated by Ora Haley for the President to ride. He's declared that after this march, nobody will ever be allowed to ride him again."

"Fascinating," said Gus, but he really wasn't interested in that kind of pomposity. In fact, realizing that he wasn't going to have the opportunity to again shake hands with his benefactor, he was ready for the celebration to be over.

He was ready to get back to his daily life at the office, posting the mail, listening to Miss Minnie's family yarns, and nudging the ink bottles.

Malachi Smith had already gone back home to Michigan, and Bill Ellison was working on a new project for his boss at Yellowstone Park. The John Bartlett affair was officially closed.

But as Gus watched the President greet the select men joining him on stage, something bothered him and that sense of duty and alert watchfulness gripped him again.

"Why so down in the mouth, boy?" said Landry, loud over the sound of the crowd.

"I'm hardly down in the mouth," said Gus.

"Reece is right," said Bess. "You seem to have something on your mind."

Gus scratched his head, tried to sound casual, but his words came out fast. "Thinking about what Smith told us, the night the hotel blew up."

"He told us he'd wasted a good bit of time," said Bess.

"No, no. He told us he'd followed Bartlett all around the country. He specifically mentioned a couple places in particular, though I can't remember them now."

"What does it matter? Bartlett is dead."

"It probably doesn't matter. It's just a detail I can't sew up."

"Look," said Bess, indicating the stage. "There's Seth Bullock beside the President."

Gus watched as the famed Dakota lawman took his place in Roosevelt's riding party next to Senator Francis Warrant, Albany County Sheriff Boswell, a few U.S. Marshals, a local stockman, and a new man, just behind Bullock, who looked oddly familiar.

"I'm surprised you didn't worm your way into that group, Landry," said Bess.

The marshal laughed. "Those men don't need me. Any one of them would be enough to protect our Lester McGurk."

"Even the Senator?"

Landry gave her a polite shrug. "Why not?" he said.

Gus wished he shared their carefree optimism. As he watched the entourage, all dressed in riding gear, wave their hats and prepare to join their horses, his attention was again caught by the eleventh man.

Gus was sure he'd seen him before. But where?

He spoke into Bess's ear. "Do you know that fellow on the end? The one in the wine-colored jacket?"

Bess nodded, "A local cattleman. Martin Clegg. He and his uncles founded half the ranches in the Sandhills, then came to Wyoming and started doing the same."

If Bess was correct, maybe he'd seen Clegg earlier that day, or the night before when they'd arrived in Laramie for the festivities.

But Gus didn't think Bess was correct.

"I'd like a closer look," he said and, nodding to his companions, moved through the crowd. When he got to the edge of the stage, he saw Clegg preparing to mount a sleek roan mare. Before doing so, he turned to speak to a boy who held the reins and Gus got a clear view of the man's face.

His dark eyebrows.

His waxed blonde mustache.

At that moment, Gus knew exactly where he'd seen Martin Clegg before and the air went out of him with a gasp. Suddenly he remembered what Malachi Smith had said about following Bartlett.

Spinning on his heel, he nearly toppled Bess as she came up behind him.

"Quick," said Gus. "Where's Landry?"

"Why, he's — ," Bess turned back the way she came. "He's there, talking to one of the University professors."

"We need to stop this ride. We need to stop it now."

"But they're already leaving," said Bess.

Gus turned. Even as he strained his neck to see above the cheering spectators he could hear the whoops and thundering hooves as the President's eleven galloped off, heading for the open range.

"It's not over, Bess."

"What's not over?"

"The John Bartlett affair. That man you think is Martin Clegg — he's not what he seems."

"I don't understand."

"There's no time. We need to get Landry."

He grabbed her hand, pulled her rapidly toward the Marshal, and did his best to fill her in.

"This man, Clegg came into the office the same day that Bartlett came to town. The same day as the hotel fire. But he didn't call himself Clegg. He called himself Augustus Butler and posed as a drummer from the east."

After pulling Landry aside, Gus shared his story with both of his friends.

"Did he say or do anything that aroused your suspicion?" said Bess.

"Assuming a false name and occupation isn't suspicious?"

"You didn't know it was false then. I mean, did he say anything at the time?"

"I think I'd remember something like that. He seemed like a perfectly ordinary customer in that he came in and asked for stamps. Made polite conversation. That was that."

Gus snapped his fingers. "I do recall he mentioned attending the World's Fair in Buffalo."

Bess gripped Gus's arm tightly. "Buffalo? What did he say?"

"Just that he had been there, that it had been an exciting time —"

"Exciting?"

"Auspicious is the word he used. And life-changing."

"The World's Fair in Buffalo is where Czolgosz shot the President."

"There's something else," said Gus. "Do you know the route Mr. McGurk's company is currently taking to Cheyenne?"

"More or less. They'll change horses a few times, stop for lunch, arrive at Fort D.A. Russell northeast of Cheyenne."

"Will they stop at a place called McGee's Ranch? Or somewhere on the Crow Creek?"

"McGee's ranch is on Crow Creek," said Landry.

"We've got to ride," said Gus, letting the

urgency flow into his voice. "We've got to ride now!"

Landry called in a couple favors and was able to procure three horses for them.

A half hour after the President's party left for Cheyenne, Gus, Bess, and Landry followed at a gallop. Still dressed in their celebratory best, Gus and Landry had only taken time to strap on holsters at the shoulder and hip respectively. Bess had taken the privilege of changing from a formal violet dress into a cotton shirt and riding britches. She carried a lever-action Winchester in her saddle boot.

Landry thought he knew a cutoff, so he led them through a series of high granite rock outcroppings toward the south fork of Crow Creek. Blooming anew with emerald grass and wildflowers of lavender and gold, the range was breathtaking. Here and there tall bunches of rusty dry grass lined their route and thick rows of pine and ivory-sheathed aspen blocked their progress.

When, after more an hour's hard ride they neared Crow Creek, Landry signaled them to reign in atop a high bluff that overlooked a deep weedy thicket.

"Other side of that gorge is the boundary for McGee's Ranch. We get through here, we turn back down Lester McGurk's route and meet them coming."

"How do we know Clegg — or Butler — hasn't already struck?" said Bess.

"We don't," said Gus, "but I'm going to assume he wouldn't endanger his own life in front of a crowd. Especially the bunch of tough lawmen he's riding with."

"I were him," said Landry, "I'd break away from the group. Maybe try and get to a high vantage like this and take out my target with a long gun."

"That does make more sense," said Bess.

"What do you suppose Bartlett was doing out here all those weeks ago?" said Gus.

"Looking for a good spot? Scouting a position to fire from?" said Landry.

"Seems if Clegg is the trigger-man, he'd be doing that himself."

"What if they were working together?" said Landry.

"Bartlett was a munitions man. He wasn't a shooter. In the end, it was his downfall," said Bess.

Gus had an idea.

"It bothers me that Clegg was in Moose-trail under an assumed name the same day Bartlett was killed. And this was after Smith had followed Bartlett around the Crow Creek area." Gus looked at Bess. "You said that Lester McGurk's route was more or less public information. What if Bartlett wasn't working alone? What if he was working for somebody?"

"Somebody with deep pockets?"

"Like Clegg's family?"

"What if his job was to sabotage the route — this route — ahead of time?"

"And once he was finished —"

"He'd arrive in Moosetrail to receive instructions or pay. Or both."

"Oh, he got paid alright."

"You think Clegg blew up the hotel in order to keep Bartlett quiet?"

Gus nodded. "The idea that an expert with a reputation like Bartlett would blow himself up —"

"Doesn't make a lot of sense," agreed Landry. "But it makes a satisfying end to the case."

"While meantime, Clegg travels with the President and sets off the charge at the specified point."

"Charge?" said Bess.

"The munitions that Bartlett planted weeks ago." Gus let his arm sweep across the horizon. "All these granite piles, all these ravines and spotty forests. An explosion of rock could bury half the party. What a story that would make."

"To what end?" said Bess.

"To prove the inherent danger of the West," said Landry. "To refute the government's message of civilized society living peacefully in a unified, safe nation. Slow westward movement."

"Keeping the west, wild," said Gus.

"If your theory is true, where do we even begin?" said Bess.

"Right there," said Landry, nodding at the horizon.

In the distance, a group of at least ten men on horseback moved along a ridge against a background of puffy cumulous clouds and dark granite outcroppings. Granite that was distinctly pear-shaped, as Smith had reported.

"We start with Mr. Martin Clegg."

Landry passed his looking glass from Bess over to Gus.

They'd been tailing Lester McGurk's party for twenty minutes. Bringing up the rear, Clegg's wine-colored coat was easy to peg compared to the others' more or less beige attire.

"By my reckoning, they're due at McGee's place in another ten minutes. Ought to be just around that big spill of rock up ahead."

"Pear-shaped rocks," said Bess.

Gus furrowed his brow over the lens of the scope, let out a curse and slapped the rump of his buckskin. "It's Clegg," he shouted over his shoulder. "He's broken away from the others. He's making for the rocks on a cut through the cedars."

Gus leaned down into the wind, speaking quickly to the horse, overpowering its instinct, using everything he knew to encourage the beast into a fast run over uneven ground. The tall granite landmark loomed less than a mile away, and as he got closer, Gus saw Clegg in a clearing of trees pull up to the base and dismount. If the rocks were to blow with the same force as the Moosetrail hotel, debris would pelt him and the President's party both. Any closer and they'd all be buried in rubble.

Gus stopped his horse and watched Clegg scramble from one boulder to the next.

He pulled his Colt and, holding it in both hands, fired off a shot.

The useless bullet pinged away through the trees, and Clegg kept moving.

"Martin Clegg!" Gus shouted. "Stop where you are!"

Gus fired again.

No use. He was too far away.

And now a new fear gripped his heart. With his two shots, he might have alerted the President's party enough to stop them in their tracks.

They were already too close. Stopping now was the last thing he wanted them to do.

It seemed like he had a choice. Ride to the left and try to force the riders to turn tail and run (and get shot in the process by any one of the Federal Marshals in the posse). Or continue to the left and do his best to stop Clegg from whatever it was he planned to do.

Either way, his luck was running out.

He chose to ride left.

With loud encouragement, he drove his buckskin around the trees to the rocks.

Coming out on the other side, Gus saw Clegg near the top of the heap.

Holding his gun hand high, he leapt from his horse.

He'd been wrong about his luck. Apparently the villain had slipped on the smooth face of the granite and taken a fall. He sat with his back against a jagged stump, his leg bent at a painful angle.

While Gus covered the distance between them, Clegg struggled to stand.

"Martin Clegg," said Gus. "Or is it Butler?"

With that, the other man stopped trying

to straighten himself. Apparently dazed by the fall, and with the heat of the noon-day sun pounding down, he slumped back and gazed curiously at Gus.

"Butler?" he said. "Do I . . . do I know you?"

Gus leveled his pistol at the bridge of Clegg's nose.

"Why, you're the . . . postmaster?" said Clegg.

"Stand up nice and slow," said Gus, suspecting the man could do nothing more.

"What's this about, Postmaster?"

"You tell me."

Clegg's eyes betrayed him, moving sideways, then back.

Gus glanced to the right. Saw the T-handle protruding from the wooden box.

A Union and Pacific detonation switch with heavy cables running away through the rocks.

"Nice and easy," said Gus, turning the barrel of the gun in a circle. "Stand up and keep away from the plunger."

"I don't know anything about that thing," said Clegg. "Whatever it is you think I'm doing here — well, I'm not."

"Stand up!" said Gus. "I won't ask you again."

"I'm just scouting ahead for the President," said Clegg. "Just . . . argh!" He winced in pain as he pushed himself to rise. "Just following up on a . . . potential threat."

Suddenly Clegg's hand whipped around, tossing a baseball sized granite projectile that hit Gus square on the collarbone. Pain pounding through his shoulder, Gus dropped his Colt, watched helplessly as it clattered down the rocky slope behind the rock that knocked it free.

Gus struggled against the pain in his arm and chest but it was like moving through liquid fire.

Grunting in triumph, Clegg pushed himself to his full height, took a terrifying step toward the plunger.

"You lose, postmaster," he said.

And then the air was cut with the clean report of a carbine rifle.

Gus could only watch as Clegg landed flat on his back, mere inches from the dynamite plunger, dead before the echo.

At the foot of the monument, Bess O'Connor waved her empty hand. In the other she held her smoking Winchester pointed at the sky.

They stood on wood planks and waited for the train at the whistle stop at Willow Siding, five miles from the post office in Moosetrail, the early morning sun just clearing the distant range of mountains.

A distant whistle.

The train was coming. Bess squeezed Gus's hand and he turned to face her.

"I don't think I ever thanked you," he said. "Not personally, I mean. For stopping Clegg. For saving us all."

"Just doing my job," she said.

"I just wish we could tell everyone." He stared directly into her green eyes. "I wish everybody knew what a hero you are."

"Oh, pooh," she said. "You know better."

Gus had to admit he did. Already, the papers were reporting the President's successful cross-country ride with ten — not eleven — men, and how it had come off like clockwork.

"History won't remember the society of the Friends of Lester McGurk, will it?" he said.

"Not if we do it right," she said.

"And now?"

"You stay here. Keep an eye on Box 13."

"You?"

"Now I go home," she said.

"Where you have your own Box 13?"

"Every town has a Box 13," she said.

Gus thought about her words.

Let them soak in and held her hand as the

train pulled around the bend.

He didn't kiss her good-bye.

That could wait until next time.

ACKNOWLEDGEMENTS

Several of the stories herein were first collected in two digital editions: Devils Nest and One Against a Gun Horde.

"Last Day at Red Horizon" and "Borrowed Time" appeared in slightly different versions at The Western Online.

"West of Noah" appeared in the Western Fictioneers anthology *Under Western Stars.*

Thanks to Wayne D. Dundee, John D. Nesbitt, James Reasoner, Bill Crider, Larry Sweazy, Peter Brandvold, Dean Wesley Smith, Dianna Graveman, Ron and Lynda Scheer, Ryle Smith, and Brett Battles.

Additional thanks to a swell bunch of hombres: David Cranmer, Charles Gramlich, Matt Pizzolato, Dave Lewis, Cap'n Bob, and the whole durned Owlhoot gang.

If you liked the stories in this book, please consider writing a short review at Amazon, Barnes & Noble or Goodreads.

ABOUT THE AUTHOR

After growing up on a Nebraska farm, **Richard Prosch** has worked as a professional writer and artist while in Wyoming, South Carolina, and Missouri.

His western crime fiction captures the fleeting history and lonely frontier stories of his youth, where characters aren't always what they seem and the wind-burnt landscape is filled with swift, deadly danger.

In 2016, Richard won the Spur Award for short fiction given by Western Writers of America.

Stop by and say hello at: www.RichardProsch.com, and be sure to join the newsletter posse or drop a line: richard@richardprosch.com

The employees of Thorndike Press hope you have enjoyed this Large Print book. All our Thorndike, Wheeler, and Kennebec Large Print titles are designed for easy reading, and all our books are made to last. Other Thorndike Press Large Print books are available at your library, through selected bookstores, or directly from us.

For information about titles, please call:
(800) 223-1244

or visit our website at:
gale.com/thorndike

To share your comments, please write:
Publisher
Thorndike Press
10 Water St., Suite 310
Waterville, ME 04901

CPSIA information can be obtained
at www.ICGtesting.com
Printed in the USA
BVHW040012090623
665670BV00001B/9

9 781432 899783